Magi

Magi

an anthology

Edited by Debz Hobbs-Wyatt, Gill James and Fatima Khan

Bridge House

British Library Cataloguing in Publication Data

A Record of this Publication is available from the British
Library

ISBN 978-1-917854-10-8

This edition published 2025 by Bridge House Publishing
Manchester, England

Contents

Introduction

The annual Bridge House anthology is always released around Christmas time. It is known for a theme appropriate to the season, while being open to subjective interpretation. This year was no exception.

When I first settled on this theme, my initial thoughts were *three wise men* or *the three kings*. However, after further consideration, we opted for the more mystical name associated with this – the Magi. We felt this encompassed more, and who says there were three, or they were all male?

Magi, in Christian tradition, refers to the noble pilgrims who followed the star from the east to Bethlehem. Christian theological tradition claims that Gentiles as well as Jews came to worship Jesus. Eastern tradition sets the number of Magi at twelve, while Western tradition sets it at three, probably based on the three gifts of gold, frankincense and myrrh.

We were excited to see how writers would interpret the theme and we were not disappointed. The selection process seems to get harder every year and the standard gets higher. It's also nice to see so many submissions coming in from outside the UK now. Of course, it goes without saying, it's also exciting for us when we uncover the name of the writer, having read, considered, shared, and finally decided we want the story, to see one of the familiar names from our family of regular contributors. And we do like to think of it is as a family of writers supporting writers. A family that grows every year.

All of these stories have taken the theme and interpreted it in a different way, some in a more traditional sense than others. The decision on which stories to include also depends on how well the story fits together and so Gill and I work tirelessly, comparing our notes once we have decided. The result is this special book you get to finally hold in your hand.

So, please sit back and feast on the stories in this collection. Maybe even consider contributing to next year's collection. Don't forget to drop us a review. Bridge House is an independent press, and supports the work of new and established writers and over the years have given voice to so many. The annual collection is where it all started and this year, like all the others since the first collection in 2008, we rely on you to read, support and share. And most of all, enjoy.

Debz Hobbs-Wyatt

Adoration

Diana Powell

She sees her in the final room of the hall – a space few visitors reach, overwhelmed, by then, by the flamboyant colours, the impatient elbows, by the spectacle. The painting hangs in the corner. The lighting is dim, as if the organizers had become weary of the whole panoply... or were deliberately trying to hide it. And the work is not big... not like the Rubens or the Lippi, who shout "Look at me! Look at me!" (Size matters to some men, in paintings, as in everything). But there is no doubt. A woman.

Of course, there has been the Madonna – what else would there be in this exhibition devoted to the Adoration? Madonna and child, haloed, illuminated, drawing the eye and the gasps of the onlookers. Mother, after mother, after mother. And an occasional nun. A procession of female martyrs, once... some of the eleven thousand, depicted in Lochner's altarpiece. All seeming to say "this is woman, this is what a woman must be". All a woman can be.

But, otherwise, it has been all men. Until now.

This, too, is a conventional scene, from medieval and Renaissance art. Joseph, on the left, then Mary, with baby Jesus on her lap, while the three magi gather round, bearing their gifts.

There is some activity in the background, but it is hard to tell what – riders, soldiers, perhaps? It is irrelevant. It is the tableau that matters, the youngest of the three "kings" who matters... to her.

For here, finally, is a female magus: a sage, a seer. One who covets knowledge, surveying the heavens, the earth; who travels the lands, in the pursuit of that learning, one

9

who belongs to a superior caste... while belonging to no-one.

Staring up at the picture, she studies the youthful face, noting the delicate bone structure, the cupid's lips, set in rounded cheeks; the pallor and smoothness of the skin. She sees the way the combed hair curls under, at the shoulder, the arched eyebrows, the length of the neck. Such feminine features... Yes, she is sure, and is glad.

No!

The voice starts up again – the voice that accompanied her, as she trailed from room to room, telling her the story of those three kings, of their depiction in art, of the inherent symbolism.

So much symbolism in it all! "The visual art of each age reflects the dynamics of the society prevalent at that specific time". Explaining how there were few "facts" to work from... how it was not even certain that there were *three* wise men. But "three gifts" were mentioned in Matthew, and there were three established continents in the world, Europe, Asia and Africa, with their three root races. Hence, the appearance of a Black Magus from early on. And life-span is often divided into three – the old, the middle-aged, the young...

... the young.

The voice whispering in her ear tells her about *this* youngest magus, now. The voice, inserting itself into her head, trying to twist her thoughts in another direction from where they want to go, away from her own conviction. A male voice, speaking in even tones, as he has done all morning. On and on and on. Blah, blah, blah. Speaking with total confidence, with authority – well, he is gallery's expert on the subject, according to the catalogue – not a hint of uncertainty in what he pronounces. And "pronouncements" are what they always are. Declarations. Not possibilities. No "maybe it could be this" or "perhaps we can see it another way". Declaring that the third king, the youngest king, is just that – a young man, personifying the early stage of adult life, as opposed to the old magus, and the middle-aged. "A familiar grouping, similar to many we have encountered in previous paintings. A typical representation, with the oldest, closest to Jesus, with his grey hair, long grey beard and wrinkled brow. Above him stands the magus in the prime of life – shorter beard, thicker brown locks. And, on the right of the group, the youngest. We can tell he is young, because he has no facial hair..." And here he – it, the voice – laughs, actually laughs, a strange noise to jump from the headphones into her ears, making *her* jump, before continuing his proclaiming. "And yes, he has feminine traits about him, which causes some to think that he is a woman, but that is incorrect. All the magi were men – could have been no other, in biblical, historical or artistic interpretation."

This, again. She has heard it before. She has been told it by her professor, in the same kind of voice as the expert who is speaking to her, through cushioned, plastic discs. The speech of another who believes he knows it all (he is the Professor of Art and Art History in a top university! He has published papers and books on the subject!). Words that resonated from the front of the lecture hall, or across the table in tutorials – or from his notes on her phone, that she has scrolled through all morning. There has never been any room for debate in his classes – there was no debate the day they studied the Lorenzo Monaco painting. As soon as it was put up on the screen, all the girls in the class starting whispering to each other, all saying the same thing – that the youngest magus was a woman. On that occasion, it wasn't just the face, circled by her braided hair – it was everything about her. The shape of her body, echoed by her

11

dress, the smock gathered beneath her breasts, then flowing down. The style and colour of her garments. Her hands... the delicacy of those hands...

...their hands, going up, then, all waiting, wanting to voice their thoughts – she among them, keen, as ever. Keen, particularly, because she had done some research into the subject, and had learnt that there was compelling evidence for the existence of female magi, from several reputable sources.

There was a laugh, then, too. Another man's laugh. Professor Cole's laugh, knowing what they were thinking, ready to deliver his punch line... actually saying those words: "I know what you're thinking. But you're wrong. Monaco was a monk, and a monk would never include a female magus. He could never entertain the idea of one – because, of course, there were none!"

A muffled buzz on her phone. A message, flashing across the professor's notes. James. Another man breaking into her thoughts, demanding her attention, as he always does. They are supposed to be meeting for lunch. He wants her to come NOW. He has found the perfect place to eat. "See you in 10!" Again, there is to be no discussion. He assumes she will do as he says.

And, of course, she should be grateful to him. She wouldn't be in Cologne, if it wasn't for him. She had told him about the exhibition in the Cathedral, celebrating the Magi. (How strange, she thinks, that the relics, the remains of the three kings ended up here! Or so they believe... the believers believe). And she had told him how relevant these paintings were to her course, how they were studying the Adoration at the moment; it is a subject she wants to pursue. It wasn't a hint; it had just been conversation. But she hadn't been surprised when he suggested they flew here for the weekend. It was the sort of thing he did. Kindness, she should think. Except... more and more, she feels these gestures are meant as a display of his wealth, of his... power. A way of telling her "this is how your life could be if you marry me". Because, lately, he has mentioned marriage several times. And children. Another more important conversation they should have... Perhaps she shouldn't have said "yes" to his invitation. But here she is.

And it is her turn to laugh, now, as the voice in her ears drones on, and James texts again. And again (because she has not replied straight away. He always likes her to reply straight away). And her professor's notes reel onto another page. She laughs, because, at this moment, it is as if she has three "wise" men in her life. Or, at least, men who think they are wise – certainly more knowledgeable than her. And she laughs, because they, by some strange chance, share the iconography of the magi. Her professor, the older man, with his grey hair and beard; James, close to middle-age; and the voice... he is a young man, from the way he speaks and from the photo in the catalogue.

Yet if he is young, surely he knows "youth" doesn't look like the third magus. And she thinks, again, "this is a woman"... just as all the female students thought it that day, looking at the Monaco picture.

She pushes her phone deep into her bag and removes the headphones from her ears.

She is still the only one in this room, and she is glad. She wants to look at the painting in more detail, without interruptions from wise men, or crowds.

She sees what she had seen, before – the face of the youngest, with its maidenly features. But there is another anomaly attracting her attention – all the figures are looking at the Christ child, except for this one. His mother, Mary, his father, Joseph, the middle king – these are gazing down, in Adoration, while the oldest king, who is on his knees, fixes his eyes above him, also in Adoration. For that is what it is about.

Yet the woman magus (yes, she will call her that!) is looking... where? Upward... where? At the roof of the building (the stable)? Beyond that... the sky, the star in it? Perhaps.

True, this is not unique (in a few paintings, one of the magi may be interacting with something else happening in the scene). But it is unusual. And it is curious that the woman seems to be averting her gaze, away from the Madonna and babe... as if she simply doesn't want to see them.

Why would this young woman not want to look? What has happened to *her* Adoration? *They* are the reason for her journey... why she has travelled so far, in difficult circumstances, while bearing such a valuable gift... to pay homage, to honour them. She is supposed to be filled with wonder at the sight of the mother and child... and yet she stares at the sky.

Could it be that she doesn't want to accept the glory of *this* maternity, because she doesn't want to allow it in *any* maternity? In her society, this is all a woman is supposed to be – a mother. This is what she should be, like her own mother before her, like her sisters, like all her female relatives, her friends. And she has worked so hard to be "other". She has left her family, she has spent so many, many hours in study, she has had to disguise herself in a man's clothing to travel freely – indeed, she has had to pretend she is a man! And yet here it is again, paraded before her again – the miracle of motherhood, the baby to be worshipped. Before she set out, she had failed to understand how confronting this image would be… how the power of it would not be denied or ignored. But, for a moment, at least, she has to look away.

Is this what the painter was trying to say? But how could a painter of that time imagine this, and want to express it in that distant gaze?

It is then that she realises she doesn't know who the artist is. The "voice" hasn't mentioned a name, neither has her professor in his notes. Who painted this strange "Adoration"?

She looks at the card on the wall, at the side of the work. Anonymous. Or… a Master of Glasgow, because that is where the work is usually held. Or… possibly… Johannes Hispanus… or… maybe not. An artist who could be anyone…

If they call me anything, they will call me "Johannes". An easy change – Johanna to Johannes – because they cannot believe that I may be a woman. And my surname will be the country I come from, or have lived in… where I painted most. But, yes, perhaps, they will not go that far. Perhaps I shall be nameless, anonymous. "Anonymous", yes! They will pick according to their reckoning, their scholarship, their "wisdom". All of which will state that 'it cannot be a woman who painted this… who painted any picture. Women cannot do that. They cannot study, they cannot travel to learn from the masters. More to the point, they cannot create. They do not have the imagination nor the discipline for that.

It is the same with the magi. The magi must be men. Wise men. Learned, rich, well-travelled men. Kings, even. But not a woman, never that.

And so I put her in there. I put "me" in there. Yes! I painted her, to mirror me… or like enough. The same hair,

15

the same eyes, the same lips. A gesture, I thought. A nod to my sex. True, I dressed her in clothing suited to the times, similar to the garb of the second magus, but that was not so different from what I myself did, as I travelled about. It was easier – easier, as in more practical; easier, to avoid... to avoid many things. Complications...

Still, I knew how it would be, when they saw my painting. "They" being those who judged these things, the masters, the rich patrons, who wanted such works to hang on their walls... who – some among them – would require their own faces to feature in the artist's impression! The Church elders. The Patriarchy. All wise men, who thought they knew everything, who decided what should feature in a painting of the Adoration. Deciding on three kings, though the Bible does not say so. Choosing the names of those kings – Caspar, Melchior and Balthazar. Deciding on their age – old, middle-aged, young. Deciding where they came from... so that, at some point, a Black magus should be included, as befitting those distant lands.

But not a female magus. No. The woman can only be the mother, the Madonna. The only one of any significance. Gaze upon her and her child, and worship at her feet!

Perhaps that was why my magus looks away. Perhaps that is why I painted her staring upwards, and not at Mary and the babe. Strange, but it happened almost without my knowledge. It was only after I had put my brush down, and stood back, that I realised what I had done, by which time it was too late to change it. And, indeed, I found I had no desire to do so. For it was "me", again, – more symbolism, depicting how I was... quite different from the symbolism of the arbiters of art. It stood for how I had been, since I was grown. Never wanting to dangle the babes of my older sisters on my knee, and "oh" and "ah" at them. With no desire to marry young, and have children of my own.

Always looking away from the domestic scene, constantly paraded in front of me. I wanted to do nothing other than go out into the world and paint. Art was the only thing I wanted to worship. My own Adoration.

What will the wise men of art say about the young magus's unorthodox gaze... if they notice, which they surely will? It is their purpose to scrutinise each piece, for both merit and meaning – and for its adherence to their conventions. They will not allow it to be a look of evasion, of that I am certain... to ignore the Madonna and child cannot be permitted! So, instead, "he" will be looking at something else. The star, perhaps, thanking it silently for leading them here. Or... God? Perhaps "he" is praising God in his Heaven for allowing this wondrous event to come to pass. And yes, "the artist has chosen to capture this look – a momentary look, before he turns his gaze back to the only subject worthy of veneration on this Earth".

Perhaps... or not. It is not always easy to predict what such men will decide.

Yet I could imagine their comments about my third magus, my youngest, the semblance of my "self", a portrait of "me"! They would say that some young men could have such an appearance – indeed, this was a way to portray them... what an artist must do. The clear skin, the lack of facial hair signified youth – together with shorter hair, because hair grew with the years, until the opposite, its loss, took place. And fine features, before the sun and the flesh took their toll. The bloom of youth! Here it was! Nothing else!

Yes, this is what they will assert about my Adoration – a declaration, brooking no denial, in the same manner as their assertions that the artist is a man. And they will say it about any other work, where the young magus has the countenance of a woman. Down, on, through the years.

17

Until... maybe... maybe... sometime in the future, a far future, a wise woman will look at my painting, and know.'

... or no-one. Anonymous. Still... perhaps. Just as she is sure the young magus is a woman, couldn't the artist be a woman, too – copying her own face, her own perspective on life, in the picture?

A position that reflects her own.

For she realises she hasn't enjoyed this exhibition, where there have been no female artists represented (well, her "wise men" would say, there were none at that time, which, again, is not strictly true.) And she hasn't enjoyed looking at painting after painting full of men, except for a mother and baby, stealing the show. Endlessly adored. Like her imagined Johanna, it is not what she wants in her art or her life.

With one last look at the painting, she heads back into the other rooms of the exhibition hall, through the crowds who continue to gaze in awe at the Adoration. As she leaves, she tosses the headphones back into their basket, and the catalogue into the bin. And she deletes her professor's notes from her phone.

James has messaged again, and again, because she didn't go to meet him, at the time he suggested. She's not going to go. She's going to walk along the Rhine, instead. And think.

She wants to think about changing her course, to another university, another professor – there is one she knows of, with a woman chair. And she must plan that conversation with James, which won't be easy, but it has to be done.

And, most of all, she wants to think about a painting.

18

Not the Adoration that she has just seen – Johanna's, she has decided – but one that is taking shape in her mind. A painting with not just one female magi, but three. One she will paint herself. Will sign for herself, in bold letters. So there will be no doubt.

About the author

Diana Powell is an award-winning writer of short fiction. Her stories have featured in a number of competitions, including the 2022 Bristol Prize (winner), the 2020 Society of Authors ALCS Tom-Gallon Award (runner-up) and the 2019 ChipLit Prize (winner). Her work has also appeared in a number of anthologies and journals, such as *Best (British) Short Stories 2020*.

Longer work includes, most recently, a novel, *things found on the mountain*, (Seren Books) and a novella, *The Sisters of Cynvael*, which won the 2022 Cinnamon Literature Award, and was published by the Press, last year.

https://dianapowellwriter.com

A Royal Dilemma

Jane Spirit

Even as I write, I cannot make sense of all that has happened to me since last night. Nevertheless, I am certain that the arrival here this afternoon of three tired travellers seeking refuge was decreed by divine intervention. I recall now how they and their small retinue of servants were allowed to enter our gates, and then greeted as guests as is customary here. How weary and dishevelled the old men looked. The remnants of the fine robes which they must have worn as they set out on richly saddled camels were now faded by constant wear. The once bright scarves still wrapped around their heads were tatty with constant ravelling and unravelling during many nights of restless sleep in makeshift camps as they traversed the empty plains. I was struck even more forcibly by their obvious friendship, the alignment of mood and the gentleness between them. It made me feel yet again how lonely I have been all my life. Oh I have had would-be followers, admirers, lovers, sycophants, but never anyone I could be sure only sought my company because they truly cared for me as perhaps only a parent or sibling can; instinctively, protectively, because they had known me since I could only crawl on dirt floors and weep at the loss of some whittled wooden doll with gauged sockets for eyes and a thin piece of pelt lashed on for hair.

Not that I could ever complain to those around me. After all I have always been the fortunate one. No whim of mine has ever been treated as ridiculous. If I wake in the night and crave the sweetness of honey, some poor soul will be sent to rouse the royal apiarist who pauses only to slip on his sandals before rushing to the hive he knows to have the most promising yield. He will barely have time to don his apron and leather gloves before he thrusts his hands into the nest and extracts a dripping cone, scraping the golden harvest into the glass vessel from which I will taste it, its thick liquid glinting in the sacred light of the moon whilst the angry bees buzz around him inflicting their dying stings on him.

I will raise the honey glass to my lips to taste its complex sweetness with no gratitude and quite content to sip only a drop or two before waving it away with a restless hand and turning instead to the plate of sweetmeats always left by my bedside. I will spare no thought for the beekeeper, just as I have no concern about the taster who risks his life daily for my preservation, or for the cook, the dresser, the whole retinue of servants, not even for the suites of soldiers who have vowed their allegiance to me though they have never met me. I have no thought of them because I have no reason to care for any one of them especially. There has never been an expectation that I would. My father died in battle before I was born, and my mother died at my birth. I was proclaimed as King when in my cradle, under the protection of my uncle who seems scarcely to have noticed me as I grew. Unbending in his apparent loyalty, he remains fixed with his stiff manners and clipped instructions. He has kept me safe, but he has never placed an arm around me in affection or reined me in when he watched me mistake tyranny for authority.

And now I feared what he might do next. I had caught a glimpse of his face earlier in the courtyard as he turned his head away from the old men who staggered with exhaustion as they dismounted. His eyes held the same hard expression as earlier when he had told me that we must rid ourselves of the girl who had entered our midst. She was a witch who had clearly contrived to rob me of my reason, he had insisted. I saw then that he was suspicious also of these star gazers and that he would have been happier to see them expelled from our safekeeping into the roaring winds and wild rain of the oncoming darkness. Might he go so far as to plot their permanent disposal, just as he was intent on destroying the young woman whose previously unknown existence had brought me so much joy and such awful perplexity?

She had come to court only yesterday evening with a troupe of entertainers from a neighbouring district. She was there, suddenly in front of me as I sat at table. I barely noticed her at first as my mind was elsewhere but then she strode forwards as if to catch my eye, to dance, to sing with only a gentle harp for accompaniment plucked from a dark corner of the room. Her voice commanded me, and I found myself mesmerised by her swirling costume, dark hair, and intense gaze. When the music ended and her clear voice faded away, I asked her a few questions out of politeness and a niggle of compassion for her blindness and the slight swelling of her belly that indicated an unborn child within. Her half-lidded eyes remained staring at me and then suddenly she reached across the board and grasped my wrist firmly, reaching into her dress to toss before me a tatty looking parchment rolled and tied with a piece of yarn. Almost before the Lords around me had sprung to their feet to protect me from an apparent threat, she had stepped back from me and surrendered herself to them to be taken away. My uncle had rapidly approached me. Perhaps it was the whiteness of his face more than the insistence in his entreaty that I have no more to do with the woman and her scroll, but somehow his objections made me determined to read the parchment. I snatched it up and left the dining chamber before anyone else could distract me, hurrying through the passages that I knew so well to find a quiet niche where I could finally hide myself, unfurl the parchment and read whatever the dancing girl had risked her life to bring me so directly.

Instantly I understood. The letter purported to be from the nurse who had attended my mother at my birth and who was now a very old woman. She told me the story of how I had been born, and that I had been, in fact, the second child, arriving after my twin sister. It had been my uncle's decision that, as my mother lay dying, the sister whose eyes seemed locked slightly open and unseeing, should not be allowed to claim her birth right. If the Empire were to be kept strong, a son should be hailed as King and a blind girl baby be disposed of. The nurse had been issued with commands to that effect and hurried to obey. As agreed with my uncle, who paid her handsomely, she had followed his plan to swaddle the baby before smuggling her beyond the walls and suffocating her. The nurse had indeed carried the girl baby away but then had secreted her alive far from court. She had raised the child as her own and eventually told her how she came to be living still and who her brother is.

I knew of course that the letter told me the truth. The girl bore a resemblance to me that had struck me as soon as I had raised my eyes to see her. Nonetheless, at dawn I emerged speedily from my curtained hidey-hole. As soon as I could find my uncle, I feigned my distrust of the girl, agreeing with him that it would be best to have her executed as soon as possible, before any gossip could emerge to weaken my rule. I also persuaded him that we should wait until the dead of night to have the deed carried out as inconspicuously as possible. Having gained some time to contemplate the situation, I spent the day alone, my agony made worse by my awareness that, in a way, my uncle is right. If the status quo is to continue the girl must be silenced and the parchment burnt. Not to do this would surely lead to my downfall and assassination, tainted as I would be by the inevitable rumours of my uncle's murderous intentions all those years before. Yet I fear that the inevitable revelation of my sister's existence will still lead to her and her baby's destruction by others equally anxious to preserve the illusion of royal sanctity. Surely neither she nor her child, even if it were a boy, would ever be allowed to claim royal privileges; a blind dancer and her bastard offspring, what kind of figureheads would they be for a powerful empire?

Then came the arrival of the three men on their camels and their coming seemed to offer me a last hope of good counsel. I waited only a short time before seeking their company in the room allocated to them in the outer fortress. There I found them both refreshed and composed. They had washed their faces and combed their beards and were warming themselves squatting before the fire I had ordered to be lit for them. And they treated me as an equal, looking me firmly in the eye. They told me their tale only once they had seated themselves comfortably on the floor cushions and welcomed me to sit down next to them. Then they explained to me that they were on their way back to the kingdoms from which they had set out variously many months earlier, meeting only after each had witnessed the revelation of the night sky whose stars they had been studying for a lifetime. The reward for their determination had been to find and pay homage to a baby who they believed would grow to be a great leader in that distant place to which the stars had guided them. They had set off back almost immediately, having become possessed suddenly of a great homesickness and strong anxiety, for their journey had come to the notice of a ruler named Herod who had seemed unusually interested in the birth foretold to them by that blessed celestial alignment. They were poor now and their supplies depleted, for they had left the child almost all the precious items they had carried with them as tokens of their devotion.

As I sat quietly with these wise men, how I longed to lay before them the truth that I had discovered. I would have spoken of my sister had not the oldest looking of them leaned forward and pressed a gnarled finger to my lips saying quietly, "I see you carry the weight of history on your shoulders, my boy, but it is best that you do not unburden yourself to us. Your story is not destined to be our story. We ask your permission to leave in a short while because we sense the danger that surrounds us here despite your own sincere welcome."

Then he stood up slowly, whilst the other two nodded their heads in agreement, and moved towards the saddlebags placed in a corner of the room. There he extracted precious paper and writing equipment before kneeling and handing it to me as a gift. "We will leave silently before the night closes in," he continued, "but before that there is time for you to write down an account of yourself for the generations to come. We will guard it with our lives in gratitude for your hospitality to us. It will be placed in our people's great library for perpetuity."

So, I have accepted the writing materials and inscribed here the tale I so wanted to tell them, of how I have found the sister I never knew I had, or rather of how she has found me. And now, in a few moments, I must go into the cell where she has been placed and speak to her. I will let her trace her fingers over my face so that she will be certain of who I am and what likeness we have to one another. What will I do next? Is it for the best that she and her unborn child die? If so, then I must have the courage to take the ritual knife I carry in my scabbard and use it well to make her death as quick and painless as I can. I cannot entrust that awful mission to anyone else. It is the one service I can do for her. But what then? Shall I take the same knife and die by it also? Or shall I turn away from harming her and instead hasten to my uncle? Shall I thank him for his wise advice before I put my arm around him with outward affection and calmly slit his throat?

This is the dilemma I face. Thanks to the kindly three men who have visited me, you who read this missive will know already the actions I have taken and how the past events recorded here have resolved themselves into a future I can scarcely imagine. I can only hope that you will not judge me harshly for what I am about to do.

About the author
Jane Spirit lives in Woodbridge, Suffolk UK and has been inspired to write fiction by going along to her local creative writing class.

Caspar's Story

Adam Joseph Mizler

My two friends and I had journeyed many miles from our lands in the East, following a star, to pay our respects to the one who was born King of Jews. The star had guided us not to a palace, but a stable in a town called Bethlehem.

The first thing that struck me, as it always did, when we made our entrance, was the menagerie of non-farmyard animals arranged around the newborn king. Zebras, elephants and lobsters were all in attendance. The second thing that struck me was that Mary and Joseph seemed to despise each other and the cordial loathing was not concealed on their faces, if you knew them as well as we did.

I was eight years old and this was our teacher's take on the traditional Nativity play, on the last day of school before the Christmas holidays. The school hall was packed with parents and relatives. I'm going back nearly forty years, so there was not a mobile phone in sight. Instead, the audience sat, rapt in the moment, fully present, waiting.

Mary and Joseph looked at us without a glimmer of surprise as we traipsed in. I was Caspar, self-appointed leader of the three wise men, the Magi. I'd been delighted to get the role, because my grandfather's name was Caspar. I thought it was some sort of divine luck that it had happened, that it meant there was forever to be this link between him and me.

It was my line now. I remembered that we were supposed to have travelled for days and nights and were tired. How the hell were you supposed to act that when the dialogue was, "We come bearing gifts for the new King of Israel. I bring gold."

There was nothing for it. I let rip.

"We have travelled from lands afar in the East. For many nights we have followed a bright star. It guided us. It brought us here to this special place."

For the first time, Mary and Joseph looked surprised.

I could see our teacher, Mr Grover, in the wings, eyes wide with what I thought must be rage as his dialogue was butchered by an eight-year-old. I decided to get back to the script. Sort of.

In my best weary voice, I said, "And though we are weary from our journey, we come bearing gifts for the new King of Israel. I bring gold."

William, up next, was trying not to laugh and just about got through his line.

I knew there'd be hell to pay for this. But in my defence, Mr Grover had not mentioned where we'd come from and he'd not mentioned how we'd got there. It was like we were just three random guys dropping in on a postnatal baby shower.

We got an applause at the end. Mr Grover made a speech. The Head Teacher made a speech. Then we were dismissed.

I hurried as fast as I could to find my family before Grover could corner me. I figured I'd at least have a chance of escaping his wrath if I was with my family. I pushed my way through the crowded hall and found my mother and father standing, waiting for me. They had a surprise.

My grandparents were there. Grandma Irene gave me her warm smile and a kiss. She was silver-haired and plump and had an unfailing optimism that was almost infectious.

Grandpa Caspar was tall and lean, with a bald crown and stringy white hair down to his neck at the back.

He gave me a rueful smile and a hug.

Then he said, "That line about coming from the East and following the star, that wasn't in the script, was it?"

I just looked at him. "How did you know?"

"It sounded… real. Not like the rest of it, clearly written by an amateur with no ear for dialogue."

"Really?"

He grinned and had that twinkle in his blue eyes that made you feel important.

My mum and dad were next with their praise and pats on the back.

"Mr and Mrs Michaels?"

It was Grover's voice.

"Mr Grover?" my mother said.

"I need to talk to you about your son and what he just did during that performance."

Here it comes, I thought.

Grandpa Caspar chimed in. "That's funny, I wanted to say the same thing."

Grover turned to him. "You did?"

"Yes, I was going to talk to him about the quality of the script. Such rich material, that enabled all the children to shine. And his line in particular, masterfully delivered, with just the right amount of weariness of someone who's made a long journey, explaining how and why the three Magi were there. It was an inspired piece of writing. Was that your work?"

Grover's mouth twitched. He hesitated. "Well, let's just say it was a collaboration." He was furious. He'd only been my teacher for a term, but I knew his facial tics well enough to know he was livid. And looking for a way out of the situation without losing face. "I'm glad you enjoyed it," was all he said as he turned and hurried through the remnants of the people who were making their way out.

I looked up at Grandpa Caspar. He smiled and winked at me.

My mum had her hands on her hips. "You shouldn't have done that, Jack." She looked at Grandpa Caspar. "And you shouldn't encourage him."

"It was the best line in the whole show," Grandpa Caspar said.

"That's not the point, dad. He can't just go off doing things he shouldn't. One day it'll get him into trouble. And you won't be there to bail him out." She stopped for a moment. "What would you do if you'd told him not to do something and he'd done it anyway?"

Grandpa Caspar said, "Well, I should hope that I would at least try to see it from his point of view and try and understand what motivated him to do it."

"I'll hold you to that next time he does something you don't like," mum said.

Grandpa Caspar smiled. A warm smile this time. I'd never seen him angry. Never seen him upset about anything. He had a cool, calm and collected way about him, as if he'd lived a thousand lifetimes and seen it all and nothing could faze him. I resolved then and there to be like that when I grew up.

"So will you come?" Grandma Irene was saying to my mum.

Dad nodded and I guessed what they were talking about.

"Are we coming to yours for Christmas?"

"Not for Christmas Day," Grandma Irene said. "But for Boxing Day. And you'll all stay over."

We were the last ones in the hall and the caretaker was starting to stack the chairs. We headed out the door and I picked up my bag on the way.

"So what do you want for Christmas?" Grandpa Caspar said.

I didn't miss a beat. "A magic set. With a real magic wand."

When I think back to that moment, I know I saw him grimace. At the time, I didn't pick up on it. I don't know if many eight-year-olds would have. But in my memory, it's

30

unmistakable that he was forcing a smile. "How nice," was all he said.

"I could bring it on Boxing Day and show you some magic tricks."

A look passed between Grandpa Caspar and Grandma Irene.

"That would be lovely," Grandpa Caspar said. Now, when I think back, I see him saying it with a false smile and his mouth twitching like Mr Grover's.

Grandma Irene looked concerned. "Are you sure?"

He nodded. "I'm sure."

"That's if he even gets a magic set," my mum said. "Santa only visits children who've been good."

I did get a magic set for Christmas. I spent all that day practising the rope-in-the-bottle trick, the hidden-card trick, the torn-five-pound-note-in-the-trick-wallet trick (this was back in the days when there was paper money and you could actually tear it) and the impossible-interlocking-rings trick.

Five tricks was plenty. I decided to wear my mum's white woollen gloves and the clip-on bow tie that someone, I forget who, had given me a few years earlier. We make the hour-long drive to my grandparents' house and arrived just before lunch. They lived in a large redbrick Victorian house, three storeys high, which had large bay windows and an impressive gable. The inside had not been decorated since the 1950s and there was a vague odour of damp in certain rooms. Nevertheless, the house was warm and inviting and the smell of Grandma Irene's cooking welcomed us as we waited at the door.

To say that Grandma Irene was a formidable cook would be an understatement. Thankfully, my mum had inherited that gene and so that Christmas, we had two delicious meals on two successive days. But I noticed Grandpa Caspar seemed a little tense. He was less his usual jovial self.

After dessert, I set up my five tricks in the living room. I put on the clip-on bow tie and then the white gloves and went into the kitchen where all the grown-ups doing the washing up.

"Step this way for the greatest magic show you've ever seen," my dad said in an overly theatrical voice.

They shuffled into the living room one by one. Grandpa Caspar was the last. He took his place in his armchair by the door. His right knee was trembling as though he was nervous.

Mum and dad sat together on the sofa. Grandpa Irene sat in the other armchair. She gave Grandpa Caspar a concerned look.

She mouthed to him, "Are you all right with this?"

He nodded.

My eight-year-old's brain thought that laughter would be the best medicine for whatever it was that was making Grandpa Caspar sad. I thought that the sight of his grandson doing magic tricks would cheer him up. After all, he'd enjoyed the Nativity Play and my ad-libbed line. A magic show would be a surefire way to lift his spirits.

I began with the tearing the five-pound note trick. I asked my dad, who I'd tipped off in advance and who'd agreed to be my plant, for the banknote. He handed it to me. I gave him the wallet from the magic set.

"See, this is an ordinary wallet, isn't it? And there's nothing inside is there?"

Dad pantomimed holding it up, opening the flaps and handing it back to me.

"Nothing inside. It's an ordinary wallet," he said with mock earnestness.

"Ah, but it's not," I said. "It's a magic wallet. And it has the power to repair damaged money!"

With that I tore the five-pound note into quarters. Grandma Irene gasped.

I placed the torn-up pieces into the wallet's main compartment.

"Prepare to be amazed…"

I smacked the wallet, opened it up and reached into the main compartment and pulled out a pristine five-pound note.

"There you are, sir, there's your money back." I said, handing the banknote to my dad.

He began clapping. Mum and Grandma Irene joined in.

Behind me, I heard footsteps. I turned, just in time to see Grandpa Caspar leave the room. The four of us stood for a moment in silence. I saw Grandma Irene bite her lower lip.

From the hall, I heard the jingle of keys, footsteps, then the door opening and closing. A moment later, Grandpa Caspar hurried past the window in his peak cap and coat and disappeared from our view. I ran to the window in time to see him step onto the pavement, turn left and hurry down the road.

Grandma Irene was behind me. She put a hand on my shoulder.

"Don't worry, darling," she said. "It wasn't you."

"What's wrong with Grandpa?"

Grandma Irene shook her head. "I wish I knew. Sometimes he gets like this. He's never liked magic shows, in all the time I've known him." She turned to my mum. "That's why we never took you to the circus or magic shows when you were little."

"When will he be back?" I said.

"I'm sure he won't be too long," Grandma Irene said.

But she didn't sound sure. "Are you going to finish your show for us?"

I didn't know what to say. I opted for the truth. "No. I think I'm going to go upstairs."

Grandma Irene squeezed my shoulder, looking out of the window in the direction Grandpa Caspar had gone. "Don't worry, he'll be fine."

To this day, I'm not sure if she was saying that to me or to herself.

I climbed the flight of stairs to the first floor, feeling as dejected as I ever had in my life. I couldn't help thinking I'd done something to upset Grandpa Caspar. That somehow, this was my fault. I was about to go into my room when I saw the stairs up to the second floor. There were only two rooms up there. A room that was used for storage. And Grandpa Caspar's study.

I honestly can't tell you what it was that compelled me to go up those stairs on that day. My eight-year-old brain had the notion that up there, somewhere, I would find the answer to what was wrong with my grandfather. There was no rational basis for this notion. It was just a feeling, like the upper storey was calling me.

I wasn't supposed to go up there. That was one of the few rules Grandma and Grandpa had. I'd been up there once, with Grandpa Caspar, to get something from his study, an old telescope and tripod that we used one night to see a lunar eclipse. That's how I knew what was up there.

I climbed the steps as carefully as I could. The wood was old and creaky, but I wasn't a heavy child and I made it up without attracting any attention. I realise now that I needn't have worried, since the three grown-ups were in the living room watching the traditional Boxing Day afternoon Bond movie.

I came to the top of the stairs. The smell of damp was stronger up here. On the left was the door to Grandpa Caspar's study, with a thick iron key sticking out of the lock. My hand was trembling as I reached out and turned it, in as slow a motion as I could. The lock clicked open and I pressed down on the wrought-iron handle and opened the door inwards.

The study was just as I remembered it from a year or so before. A single window, in front of which was the telescope, pointing upwards to the sky. On the floor, piles of papers, newspapers, boxes and cartons. On my right, a bookshelf of dusty leatherbound tomes – and a few that were from within the previous twenty years. There was a pathway between the piles of papers and the boxes that led to a heavy oak desk with a wooden swivel chair, padded with cushions and pillows. I wondered how they would have got the desk up the stairs and into the room, because the door didn't seem wide enough.

I took a deep breath to calm myself. If Grandpa Caspar came in, he'd be furious. If he ever found out I was in here, he'd be mad. I remember thinking I must have been mad to even come in here. But I decided, I was here now, so I'd have a look round and see what I could find. But I had no idea what I was looking for. And there was so much *stuff*. I put my hand to my head as I realised the enormity of the task that was ahead of me. It would take *days* to go through all of this.

I headed towards the chair and the desk, which were under the eaves, looking around as I did so. I remember thinking the best thing I could do was leave. But then I saw the brown cardboard box, with faded handwritten letters from an old marker pen, "Old mems 1930s".

I knelt down and took the lid off the box. Inside I saw a collection of photographs of people I didn't recognise, and who didn't resemble anyone in our family. They were in a variety of costumes, men and women, like actors.

Underneath was a leather book, roughly the size of letter paper. I opened it. On the first double page, in the top left-hand corner was the date, 1937. Impeccably straight vertical pencil lines had been drawn with a ruler down the pages to form columns. There were words and numbers on the page. At the top of one of the columns, in an ink pen, was the word "Earnings". To an eight-year-old, this didn't mean much, other than the obvious that whoever was writing in this book was keeping track of how much money they made. I wondered why grown-ups fussed so much about money. It seemed simple to me, who only had pocket money to worry about – you either saved it or spent it.

Then there was a column called "Venue". I had no idea what that meant, but in that column were the names of places like "Blackpool Empire" and "Blackpool Roxy" and a host of others in different places in the country, most of which I'd never heard of.

I flipped through a few more pages. To be honest, I thought it was boring. Just a bunch of places and numbers. I wasn't even sure that it was my Grandpa's, because none of the photos on top of it were of him. I put the book to one side and looked back into the box.

What I saw next shocked me.

I felt my mouth drop open and suddenly it was dry.

I blinked several times to make sure I was actually awake.

There, on top of the rest of the contents of the box, was a torn piece of paper. Most of the sheet was missing. I guessed I was looking at a quarter of it and that if it had been whole, it would have been about two feet long and one and a half feet wide. We had paper this size in school. Grover had said it was "A2 size".

It had been torn at an angle. What I was holding was the top of the sheet, which compromised the top left-hand corner and going down to about half of what I imagined the whole length would be. It was as if someone had ripped the sheet off a wall, starting at the top right-hand corner, tearing it diagonally down to the bottom left. But whoever it was had been careless. Instead of a straight diagonal tear, they'd ripped off three quarters of the sheet, leaving something that resembled the capital letter F, only without the second horizontal bar.

The paper was old and brown and made me think of the papyrus scrolls we'd learnt about when we studied Ancient Egypt that term in school. But what had struck me was not the age, or the smell of old paper, but the words that were legible.

Caspar B Melchior
One of the great
M A G I

Caspar was my Grandpa's name. But Melchior wasn't his surname. Was it?

It clicked into place in my brain in an instant.

Caspar was one of the Magi. The one I'd played in the Nativity.

And Melchior was the name of the second.

B must have been for Balthazaar, the third of the Magi.

Caspar B Melchior.

All three of them, in one name.

Beneath the words was part of a photo of my grandfather as a young man, in a strange Middle Eastern costume. The rip had dismembered his torso, but it was him, for sure.

I realised I must have been holding part of a poster. A theatrical poster, most likely.

37

I felt my heart beating faster. It had not been a coincidence that I got the part of Caspar in our school play. Somehow, I felt it was divinely mandated. I was following in my grandfather's footsteps. Long ago, he too had been in a play where he was a Magi. I was holding the proof in my hands. Maybe he played all three of them. Maybe as one single character. Why not? It would have been more interesting than what Grover had come up with.

I heard voices downstairs.

It was Grandpa Caspar.

And Grandma Irene.

I froze. Terror seized me and once again my mouth was dry.

Their voices got louder and I realised they were on the landing downstairs.

Grandpa Caspar was saying, "I just want to see him and try and explain."

"He's probably sleeping. Wait till he wakes up and comes down. Now come on, come and have a cup of tea."

I heard their footsteps go back down. Without thinking, without looking, I placed the piece of poster back in the box, placed the book on top of it and replaced the lid.

As silently as I could, I wended my way back to the door, stepped out and pulled it closed behind me. I twisted the key in the lock, praying that it wouldn't make a loud click.

No such luck.

I held my breath, imagining the click reverberating round the house and the grown-ups coming flying up the stairs.

Nothing.

I exhaled and crept down the stairs, being careful not to tread on the creaky ones.

I made it to my room, closed the door behind me and fell onto the bed.

My mind was racing. Grandpa Caspar and I shared a special link now. I couldn't wait to talk to him about it.

That's when it hit me. A new problem. I couldn't talk to him about it because that would mean I'd have to tell him *how* I knew. And that meant telling him I'd been in his room.

My heart sank as it dawned on me that I would have to keep this to myself. That I'd never be able to speak about it, with anyone. Ever.

That's just how an eight-year-old thinks of these things. With a heavy heart, I went downstairs.

The three of them were still in the kitchen. On the television, James Bond was dispatching a bad guy.

"Where's Grandpa? I thought I heard him come in."

"He's gone up to his study," Grandma Irene said. "But don't worry, he'll be down in a while. I know he wants to talk to you."

I nodded and wondered off into the kitchen. There were leftovers on plates covered with clingfilm on the table. I began to unwrap one and take out some cold turkey.

"Jack," came Grandpa Caspar's voice from behind me. I turned. "Are you all right?"

I nodded. "I'm fine," I said. But I knew I'd blurted it out too quickly and it didn't sound sincere. I quickly shoved the turkey into my mouth.

He walked over to me and looked down at me. His face was stern. "I know you're not fine. And I know it has something to do with me. Something to do with me walking out of your magic show. And I know it has something to do with this—"

In one swift movement, his empty right hand was by my left ear and in front of my eyes was the torn piece of poster. For the second time that day, my mouth dropped open. Only this time, chewed turkey fell out.

I tried to speak. He shook his head.

"I know you were in my study. The things in that box were not how I'd left them. And you were the only one with the motive and the opportunity."

I felt sick. He said, "Don't worry, I'm not angry."

"Are you disappointed in me?" I could feel tears welling up in my eyes.

"No," he said. "I think you have a question for me." He gestured with his eyes to the torn piece of poster in his hand.

"Were you like me?" I said. "Were you one of the Magi, in a play, in the olden days?"

He looked puzzled. "That wasn't the question I was expecting." He thought for a moment. "I suppose it'll do." He walked over to the other end of the table and placed the piece of poster on the surface.

"In the olden days," he said, "I was an entertainer. Singing, dancing, jokes, tricks, tumbling, clowning, you name it, I did it. And then..." He stopped. I saw he was fighting back tears. "And then I met Florence." He choked at the words.

I had no idea who he was talking about. "Who's Florence?"

"She was my wife. My first wife. We met in 1936. She was in the chorus-line at a theatre in Blackpool and I was part of a double-act called Caspar and Dickens. I thought she was beautiful. She thought I was funny. And we fell in love and got married. I have to say it, the years I spent with her were the best of my life. We were dirt poor. I took what work I could, we just about got by. I chose the name Caspar B Melchior for my act. Florence thought it sounded exotic. She was my beautiful assistant. And we were happy. We talked about having a family. And then it all changed."

I frowned. "Why?"

"Because the War came. I enlisted, but I was found to

40

have a heart condition, so I was given a Grade B, which meant I was unfit for general service. But I was fit for non-combat service and given my background in theatre, I was one of a few who spent the War entertaining the troops."

"Where?"

"All over. In the Middle East, in India, eventually in Europe. It meant I had to leave my darling Florence for months at a time. She understood, of course. She played her part volunteering with the Red Cross. And then one time, it was in August 1940, I got some leave and I went back to see her. We'd been living in London just before the War and as we didn't have any children, she stayed there. But it was incredibly dangerous. The German planes bombed the city every night. I got back just as night was falling, this one evening, and there was an air-raid. I was only a few streets away from where we lived. And I had to duck into an air-raid shelter. All the streets were pitch black, because everybody had to have blackout blinds in those days. And she knew I was getting back that evening…"

He stopped. I looked at him. But he was far away. In another time. Another place. London. August 1940. His voice was flat. As if the disbelief was so complete and total that all emotion had been suppressed.

"It was my fault. Indirectly. I'd told her what day I'd be getting back and that it'd be in the evening. And she'd been in the bedroom, sitting at her dresser, making herself beautiful for me. Maybe she didn't turn the light out in time. Or maybe she did and she was just unlucky. But the bomb fell and it was a direct hit. You know, we only had one mirror in the house. On her dresser. In the bedroom. And that's how I know she was making herself pretty for me. Because when they found her body, there was mirror-glass…"

He began to sob. I didn't know what to do. This was so

41

far out of my range of experience. I just put my arm out to comfort him and squeezed his arm. He patted the back of my hand.

"I wasn't a Magi. This is what I was…"

In his left hand, I saw he was holding a large piece of old paper. I had no idea how he'd hidden it from me. He placed it on the table. It was the missing piece of the poster. And I saw what the words actually read.

Caspar B Melchior
One of the greatest
M A G I C I A N S

The black and white photograph below the title was now complete. It showed Grandpa Caspar as a young man, posing with his hand held above his head, fingers pointing forward as if to make something appear from the hat he was holding. Next to him, a smiling young woman in a sequined dress. Probably very risqué for the time. She was pretty, with a bob of dark hair.

"Is that Florence?"

He nodded. "The day she died, the magic went out of my life. And I never truly got it back." He looked at me. "But I did when I met your Grandma. And then when we had your mum. And again when she had you." He looked down at me. "But sometimes, it's all too much. It was today, when you were doing your show. I'm sorry."

I wanted to tell him that he didn't have to be sorry. But I couldn't get the words out. There were tears in my eyes. I hugged him. He hugged me.

In my memory, that's how we remained, he and I, and how we'll always be.

I never did finish that magic show for my family and the magic set went untouched for many years before we gave it to a charity shop.

But I have the poster on my wall in my own study, now. I had it repaired and restored and set in nice frame.

That poster serves as a reminder, a reminder of two lives, two stories.

And the magic they brought into my life.

About the author

Adam Joseph has been writing fiction, both long-form and short-form, as well as plays and screenplays, for some thirty years. Under the pen name Joseph Roland, he wrote the flash-fiction story 'Red Letter Day', which won the February 2024 voice.club competition, and can be found here: www.youtube.com/watch?v=KpeP9r1hxKA. He is currently working on an epic historical fiction novel set in Jerusalem in the years 66-70CE. He lives in West Sussex, by the coast, with his wife and their cat.

Epiphany

Joyce Frohn

The two men on the hillside pulled their cloaks closer in the early morning chill. "It's been a year and a half. Do you think we still need guards all night long?"

Yosef stroked his beard. "I don't know, Benjamin. Isn't that for the council to decide?"

"That's another thing you have to change. If you're going to be the father of the next king, you shouldn't let a town council determine how you behave."

"They're wise and old and I am neither. Besides you know how 'persuasive' Herod can be. Let alone the Romans." His mind flitted from one horror to another, from the gasping rattles of the crucified men to the wet ripping sound the Roman whips made as they shredded human flesh. He remembered whispers of what even the Romans didn't let anyone see. Only rumours, no one came out alive from a Roman prison. Yosef wondered if the legends had been exaggerated. It was said that no one could keep from telling his secrets once the Romans began their foul work.

Benjamin sighed. "I suppose you're right." He laughed slightly. "It would good if you could stay."

Yosef nodded. "Yes. To be able to raise a king in the same city our greatest king came from. That would be good."

Benjamin snorted. "I meant that this town has needed a wheelwright for years, and you're one of the best. I've always hated having to get someone to come from Jerusalem." He stood and stretched. "Dust. Soldiers."

They ran down the hill. Yosef's heart pounded from more than the run. How could he have been so foolish? He should have known that there was no way to keep a secret king. Yosef wondered what kind of destruction Herod would order. Some of the elders had said that Herod might be merciful.

That was a lie. Herod had killed his own son for trying to take his throne. Herod would kill everyone in the town, and it would be his fault. Those stories of Roman prisons were probably understated. Benjamin went to round up the young men. Yosef knew they would try to mount enough of a defence to let him and his family escape. If only there were some faster way to get his family away than a donkey, but no one in the village owned a horse. He expected to hear the screams of the vanguard of the soldiers attacking young men armed with sticks and stones any second. No one could question their bravery, but a shepherd's staff wouldn't do much against Roman armour and a sling couldn't hurl a stone as far as a Roman spear could fly. What would he tell Mari? Where would they go?

Yosef had the donkey harnessed to the cart when one of the young men ran up, breathless. "It's safe." He panted. "They came to worship the new king."

"What? Do the elders know? The soldiers with them will report back to Herod and then what?"

The young man grinned. "They know. The elders say it's safe." Yosef stared dumbly at him.

Benjamin joined them. "I think it's safe. They say they understand. They're Magi –They're different."

Yosef nodded, slowly. He let Benjamin led him away. Out of the corner of his eye he saw the young man unharnessing the donkey. He rubbed his hands and stood up straight for the others. He would calm their fears even if there was no one to calm his. The crowds parted. Most of the men of the village were there. Hands reached out to touch him, to pat his shoulder or touch his hand. When the last of the crowd parted, he saw the strangers.

There were five camels, five horses, and more donkeys than he had ever seen in one place. His heart skipped a beat. There was an entire cohort of Syrian guards. A man in long, flowing robes stepped forward. His ringleted hair showed no dust, and Yosef guessed from the whisper his robe made that it was silk. Yosef was conscious of the fact that he had been up all night and was wearing the same robe he had worn for a week. The stranger had long, hennaed fingernails and a ring on each finger.

The man pressed his hands together. "Shalom."

Yosef stared. How could this stranger know Hebrew? The accent was rough, but understandable.

The stranger smiled and began to speak in Greek. "I know no more of your language. Do you speak Greek? Are you the father? Do you need an interpreter?" He glanced at Benjamin.

Yosef took a deep breath and bowed. "I speak a little Greek. I am the father." The stranger led him to richly dressed men, each of whom bowed to him. Yosef tried to remember their names, but some of them were introduced by a title and his Greek wasn't good enough to understand much. He also tried to count the scuttling servants. The poorest of them wore cotton robes finer than anything sold in this town. They moved too fast. There had to be at least two dozen. His head spun. Yosef knew who they were. The Magi, wise as Solomon, dangerous as a viper and fearful of nothing, not even Rome.

"Why?" Yosef said. "Why did you believe that the son of a wheelwright could be a king?"

It was a black man who answered. "The stars told us that you would have a king."

"Why do you find it hard to believe that you could be the father of the next king? Wasn't your last king the son of a blacksmith?"

Yosef gulped, remembering how the Maccabees had taken their throne. There had been seven sons and how many had died in combat? Their father had fallen first then the women of the family had been... How many had died in the long war? How many thousands would die in the one to come? "I will lead you to the child and his mother." He led them to the small house they were renting. He stopped at the mezuzah on the gate.

"Sir." Yosef kept moving, until he realized one of the noblemen was speaking to him. It made him a little nervous to realize that these great men could be referring to him.

He stopped and turned. "Yes?" He realized that they were all outside the gate. The one that had first spoken to him was in front.

"Do we need to touch that? Are there special words we need to say?" The man in front looked nervous. Surely, Yosef thought the great Magi weren't afraid of the Hebrew God, or were they?

"No. Only members of our religion." The whole group gave a sigh of relief and passed through the gate. Yosef felt a thrill. Maybe Israel was just a petty state in the Roman Empire, but their God was powerful and if He willed, they would be great nation again. Rome would learn that there was no opposing the God of Israel.

Yosef paused at the door. "I will tell my wife that strangers are coming." They waited outside. He slipped in and almost tripped on the naked infant Yeshua, playing in the dirt of the doorway.

"Abba." Yosef picked him up.

"Husband, I heard voices," Mari said. "Is there something the matter?" He noted how pale she looked. He wished he could keep the world away from her.

"There are noblemen outside. They came all the way from the banks of the Tigris to see our child."

Mari shrieked. "The house is a mess. My dress." She ran to the chest and got out her veil. She pawed to the bottom to get a robe for Yeshua. She took him from Yosef and dressed him. She put him down to put on her veil. He ran toward the cook fire. Yosef grabbed him.

"You'd better hold him." Yosef pointed her to the sleeping platform.

"Chickie." Yeshua waved to the wary rooster that appeared in the courtyard doorway. He struggled to get away. Yosef handed him to Mari, shooed the chicken out and shut the door. Yeshua started to cry. Yosef opened the door to the noblemen.

"My lords, my son, Yeshua." The child laughed and clapped his hands.

Three men came in first, including the black man. They entered and knelt before Mari and Yeshua. Four more men came carrying a variety of boxes. Benjamin and the Rabbi also came in.

Yosef laughed silently. Mari didn't need to worry about how the house looked. With all these people, he couldn't even see the walls. The men with the boxes opened them. Yosef gasped. He could smell frankincense and myrrh. The third box glittered with gold.

One of the strangers spoke to him. "We understand how difficult it can be to raise an army. These small gifts may be of some help. All the pieces are small enough to sell without raising suspicion."

Yosef felt the pit of stomach twist. He wished they wouldn't speak of such things in front of Mari. Women shouldn't hear about wars. All the men knelt before the child, one after the other, and placed his feet on their heads.

Yosef realized who these people were: besides the Magi, or were they Magi, too? Sabateans, who wanted to ensure their freedom from Rome; and Ethiopians, who wanted as much as the Jews did to throw off the yoke of Rome. Yeshua wasn't even two, and already allies were gathering, or alliances anyway. His poor head hurt as he tried to sort out what his response should be. If he showed greater favouritism to one than to another, would he start a war?

"Yes, Reb Daniel?" The Rabbi pulled on his arm. Yosef was hoping for some wise advice.

"Yeshua should bless them, with Aaron's blessing."

Yosef moaned at the thought. He had just gotten Yeshua through the "Shima Israel" a week ago. He dreaded trying to get the boy to repeat a more complicated phrase in Hebrew.

He pushed his way to his wife and child. Mari was looking pale. He took Yeshua in his arms. He held the boy's arm up. "Repeat what I say, Yeshua."

"Yes, Abba."

"May the Lord,"

"May the Lord." He said with only a little stutter.

"Bless you," Yosef said.

"Bless you."

"And keep you."

"And keep you. Chickie." Yeshua struggled in his arms, waving to the rooster that had slipped back in. One of the servants grabbed it and handed it to Yosef. Yeshua happily petted it.

Yosef was glad to see them all head out of his small house. The Rabbi was trying to tell him the proper rituals for cleansing the house after Gentiles had been inside. Yeshua was babbling about 'chickies,' and Mari was asking whether the frankincense, myrrh, and gold were real. Just then he felt a warm stream of liquid flowing down his leg.

It was two days later that Yosef headed to the Magi's campsite, early in the morning.

Benjamin intercepted him. "You won't find them. I was out earlier, and they had already disappeared."

49

"They were warned in a dream to leave."

"How, how do you know?" Benjamin looked shocked.

"I just know." Yosef said. "I had a dream, too. We'll be leaving as fast as possible."

"Where?"

"Egypt. Isn't there a verse about that, 'Out of Egypt I have called my son'?"

"But," Benjamin said. "There won't be a caravan to Egypt for months, and you can't travel all that way alone."

"Egypt. Exile. If anyone asks…" Yosef stared at him, hoping he understood what could not be said.

"You've gone to Egypt. I'll tell the young men that you left with the Magi. I'll miss you." They embraced and kissed.

"I'll miss you, cousin." Yosef rested his head in his hands. "Maybe it would be a good time for you to go on that pilgrimage to Jerusalem you were talking about. Maybe you should leave someone else in charge of the inn."

Benjamin bit his lip. "The rabbi and I will cover your tracks and both of us will disappear for a while. You'd better go. Women will be going to the well soon." He wiped the tears from his eyes and turned his back. Yosef hurried back to the house. Mari was finished packing. After leaving several gold coins behind, Yosef loaded everything into the donkey cart. The money seemed so inadequate as thanks for the whole town risking their lives to protect him.

After he had everything loaded into the cart, Mari carried the sleeping child out. He settled them on the pile of boxes. Yosef went into the mountains, planning to stay hidden until he could join a caravan heading somewhere. Maybe he could get to Petra, capital of Saba.

This close to Bethlehem most of the robbers were really Zealots and wouldn't attack a Hebrew king. The shepherds would have told them. Everyone knew how close the shepherds were to robbers. Come to think of it most of them were both. He smelled something, something rotten.

In a deep ravine, he saw the source of the odour; the Syrian guard that had been with the Magi. They did understand and had taken care of the guard. He could see no sighs of violence on the bodies, probably poison. Yosef hoped the scavengers took care of the bodies before the Romans or other Syrians came looking for them and took revenge on the town.

"Husband, what's that smell?"

"The Syrian guard. The Magi took care of them. They're no danger to us."

She moved to see what he meant. When she saw the corpses, she screamed. Yeshua cried. "They shouldn't have killed them. I thought you said they were kings. Kings shouldn't do things like this." Mari's words mixed with sobs.

"Men sometimes have to do things like this, kings more than most. Why, King David killed thousands of enemies—"

"No. Not Yeshua. I don't want him to do this. If he has to be a king—"

"Mama. Yeshua be good king." He reached up and wiped the tears from her eyes.

Yosef drove on. When he glanced back, he could see dust on the Jerusalem Road. He was careful to keep his face calm. It wouldn't do for Mari to know all that his dream told him.

After all there was no way to oppose the will of the God of Israel.

About the author
Joyce Frohn is married to a wonderful man. She has an adult daughter who is still hanging around. She shares a house with two cats, a guinea pig and too many feral dust bunnies.

Follow Your Own Star

Sally Angel

"Well, hello!" The young man darts forward. "*Mummy.*"

He grabs a paper hat from the overflowing table, and crams it on his head. Mel clocks the ginger hair, gelled vertically in a modern style. Where has she seen it before? The voice too hits a nerve.

"I bring gold."

Don't wake him. But it's too late. In the stroller, Oliver opens his eyes, of course he does, and blinks at the yellow Quality Street wrapper in his face. Brilliant. So much for her plan: a big dollop of Calpol – keep his lordship asleep for as long as possible. Get through today. *You can do this.*

But can she? She's not the same woman, the one that was only responsible for herself. A normal adult. Now she's in charge of another life and it's terrifying.

Ollie flings the second gift offering on the floor. He's hyped up and raring to go by now. The stroller lurches as he tries to break free from the straps.

"Third time lucky!" shouts the wise man.

Ollie's eyes gleam. Ah, shiny treasure! Small pudgy hands shoot out; a silver flash is heading, oh no, for his mouth. Mel throws herself across him, snatching the paper clip. Just in time.

"*Stupid.*"

A stutter. "Sorry.*"

Mel breathes again. Perhaps this guy doesn't have kids himself. But seriously, the wise man act is weird. Ollie's not just emerged from her womb. It's the season for barbecues and beaches, not swaddled dolls and magi.

"You made it then?"

Ah, sanity. A dark-haired woman in a suit hurries into the office. She must be the one Mel had a disjointed mobile conversation with recently. But like the ginger guy and three girls who've gathered round to Ollie-worship, she's not familiar. It's like Mel's in some past life regression. She should know these people. But they look wrong, sound wrong.

Or is it her? Has she been out of the loop too long, forgotten how to do social interaction, spent too long in her own head?

"Great to see you!" Nadiya. That's the woman's name. *But she's not my manager*, Mel's thinking. Where's Geoff?

"Taken retirement." The pretend wise man fills her in.

Retired, my backside. Mel snorts. Not Geoff. More likely he called a female colleague "dear", or committed some other faux pas he didn't know was sexist. Like her own dad might have done. Geoff had been here for ever. Ok, he was packed off on update courses for IT and Inclusivity in the Workplace from time to time, but he was the one person Mel could rely on and trust. The real deal. A true wise man. And now he's gone.

They *are* getting rid of people. In that disembodied phone exchange, Nadiya had rattled on about "gender equality… diversity quotas." And it does explain the Sorry To See You Go! banner strung above the table that's littered with half-eaten pizzas, no doubt in honour of the latest casualty.

Nadiya fetches them peppermint teas from the drinks machine, and pulls up two chairs. Not very private, but Mel sinks into hers. She's sweating and is likely to slump into sleep on the spot. But she must stay alert, to negotiate for her position, and Ollie's future. She gives him his juice bottle to keep him quiet, and dives straight in.

"Could I work at home?" No need for new clothes. No transport costs.

"*So* sorry, Mel. Quality Essentials has a strict Back to the Office policy."

Of course it has.

Nadiya's performing coochy-coochy noises at Oliver, which makes him wriggle. And is that a rumble somewhere? Mel coughs loudly. *Please let it just be a fart.*

"The thing is," Nadiya looks away. "Your job's gone."

"What?" Minty liquid splashes onto the one reasonably unblemished skirt Mel managed to find and fasten with a safety pin around her middle.

"They can't sack you," Jack had insisted, when they dug out the maternity leave document she'd never bothered to read. She knew the gist and the rules, and returning to work was months away, a world away at the time. Who knows if the law has changed. She'll just have to blag it.

"You can't get rid of me. I have rights."

"No, no. We still want you." Nadiya's trying to blot Mel's skirt with a paper towel. "It's the job *title* that's changed."

Mel goes weak with relief. She's not unemployed. And it does explain why the Marketing nameplate on the department door was missing when she came in. Whatever this is new role is, she can do it.

Whenever she needs to believe that, she thinks about visiting her grandma in the hospice when she was dying; how that wonderful lady had leaned forward. "Always follow your own star, Mel." And she had remembered that self she was deep down, understood her own uniqueness, and felt seen. Hold onto that thought.

Nadiya fetches her a tag. It's got her name on and, underneath, *Content Creator*. Well, she's that all right. After a youth of trying not to be one – no suitable partner, not the right time or situation – it's happened. At forty. Not the last tick of the clock exactly, but the moment when risk factors shoot up.

And she's done it, the ultimate creative manifestation. Is buzzing with it. You couldn't do anything more creative, messy, more stupid than bringing a new human into being. But as a job description, what the hell is it? Time for Mr Google.

"I'll just see to Oliver." This time the noises from the stroller are definitely not wind. Staff clearing up the party stuff are trying not to sniff.

In the changing room, Mel sorts Ollie's bumwear, then Googles.

A content creator is somebody who creates written, graphical, video or audio content for audiences. Blah blah blah.

Mel forces herself go back into the fray, and is struck again by how alien the workspace is, not like it was before. They've moved everything round. And as well as Geoff being gone, there's also no Rose.

Rose was always part of Mel's working day. They'd sit side by side, Rose regaling Mel with tales of The Demons, her teen kids. And then it hits Mel. The reason she doesn't recognize these employees today is because they *are* strangers. She expected everything to be stuck in a time capsule, which would make returning just about bearable. But of course it isn't.

Mel flips the brake, spins the stroller round, and starts towards the exit, ignoring the reality of what her life is now, and what her role is as a parent, a person of maturity, a provider, a carer, a protector.

"You'll have to go back." That was Jack last week, hair wild, swearing at the unpaid bills. Mel thought she might kill him. It was too early. Yes, when you procreated you had to become grownups. And she had to accept the pain along with the joy.

But this wasn't how it was supposed to be. She'd have

a year off, bond with her child, create an organised daily structure, go to coffee chat mornings with other mothers to swap experiences, and become skilled at this mummy business.

She managed some of it, but it was one step forward, two steps back. And Mel didn't know who she was now. What was her purpose? She'd lost her power. She'd lost herself.

Most post-partum friends were back at work as soon as they could go out in public without walking funny.

"Oh I couldn't stay home. I'd go mad." And there was that. No adult conversation, grabbing anyone who called. *Talk to me.* But the alternative wasn't right either, yet, for Mel.

However, the small print said otherwise. Her payments were to be reduced. A lot. They couldn't manage. Jack's parents would babymind mostly… he could work from home two days… and there was a free crèche in town on Fridays. There was no choice. So here she is.

"It's the same work, really." Nadiya's trying to block her escape. Well, she would. She knows Mel could have a case (admittedly flimsy) against *Quality Essentials,* for changing her contract details. And they'd have to train her replacement, and pay competitive rates. "Writing the storylines. And you'll be working with Nathan."

Ah, that's the wise guy's name. Mel does vaguely remember him now, but he was in a different department.

"We do free baguettes on Fridays." Nadiya's pleading now. "And can offer staff Mental Health Provision."

Well, yippee. Mel shivers at a cold wetness in her top underwear, which still happens if she's anxious, though her milk should have dried up by now. She daren't look down at her shirt, to see if there's a tell-tale patch. That's another problem. There's so many body embarrassments when you have a child, when your two roles collide. Mother and working woman.

Nadiya hurries to a planner on the wall. A fortnight today. Yes?

Mel shrugs. Two weeks, two months, two years. It doesn't matter. She's never going to be ready.

At first, it was like plunging into a body of water, not knowing if she would resurface again. Ups and down continued, as she was getting used to the external world again, being with people each day.

But she's learning to go with the flow. Harry in production, and Karl in packing are dads themselves, so don't take any notice if she's hormonal, used to it with their partners. The girls in the office treat Mel as if she's their (younger) mother. And she rubs along with Nathan because she has to.

Maybe she's not quite the old Mel yet, the self of before. But being on the edge is exhilarating. Coping on minimum sleep can be euphoric. And when things go belly up, she almost doesn't notice, because there's not time. There's the next Ollie pickup, the next work assignment, load of laundry, fumble in the night. Mothers, she realizes, have to stretch and learn to be more than they thought they could be.

I am a magician!

I am powerful.

She is woman. She can do anything.

Mel stumbles out of the meeting four weeks later. She's dazed. They're all dazed. The company has had its funding reduced. And that means one thing.

"Cuts."

It's every man or woman for themselves. Who's going and who isn't?

The younger ones, the girls in her department might be saved. They are on a lower pay scale, and they are "women". Also they are basically admin. It's the other staff, trained and experienced who will be at risk. In their department it's obvious. It's going to be herself or Nathan.

Mel might have the advantage as Nathan is male, but they have to retain some men. Or it will be reverse discrimination. Mel will stand her ground. She has to, for herself and her family. Although in a different way from today's world women, wise women, have been doing that through history.

Follow your own star. Be who you really are, in therapy-speak. Believe in yourself. So here goes.

Nadiya's beckoning to her. She's been a bit off recently, snapping at Mel. So could this be it? The chop. Nadiya takes her aside.

"Does it hurt?" Nadiya whispers.

Yes, it hurts, Mel thinks dully, that everything I try to do goes wrong. Then Nadiya looks at her and Mel sees the hollows under the other woman's eyes, the dull tinge to her skin. And she knows what she means.

"Yes, Nadiya," she says gently. "It does hurt. But you soon forget the pain." *Liar.* There is no other pain like it. It hurts like hell, and it goes on hurting, doesn't stop. And she thinks how this woman who is more educated and senior than her is asking *her* advice because Mel has an experience she hasn't yet been through.

This is the deal Nadiya tells them, when she has composed herself. *Quality Essentials* has got a contract to create a Christmas television advert. Mel and Nathan will each work on their own project, and the one that's chosen will stay with the company.

So it *is* her or Nathan. Mel can't think of a single idea.

How to think Christmas in September? Playing snowscene videos to get the vibe is not like the real thing. We need the darkness, the emotion of carols, the grotto with sleigh outside.

Mel's looked at the adverts of the big stores from previous years. It'll be two minutes at most. There's the main character with a heart – tugging Christmastime situation, and you have to show with minimum dialogue and as many products as possible, how the story is resolved.

Think Mel, think!

Nathan's over at his work station, ginger head bent to his screen. That's it! The wise man. The wise men. What synchronicity. The suppressed memory returns. Last December, she'd gone to the local school nativity play with a neighbour, tired of waiting, of being a balloon. There's the donkey arsing about, the shepherds tripping over dressing gown hems, and the three tallest boys in the school, dressed in their mums' curtains, walking… walking… she can see them – walking towards the birthing pod at Mary's feet.

Before the rip of pain.

She's back there, and excited now. Shepherds are lovely, but the Magi will utilize more products. Scented gift boxes for the presents. There can be people of other cultures, different religions. Bingo!

Mel works through the nights at home, reading books and the internet. We think we know how it happened, by heart. But there are so many stories, from different perspectives, biblical and historical. Magi, Mage, the wise women, wise men, learned, foretellers. As it all takes shape in her mind, Mel forgets the worries about the future. Whatever it holds.

She's back.

It's the evening of the presentation. Jack said he'd meet Mel there.

But she's not on her way. She's at the hospital. Oliver had a temperature and couldn't be roused. She's in the waiting room. The guilt's overwhelming. She's been caught up in her own life. Did she do or not do something vital?

Her phone pings. It's Jack sending her a video of her presentation. She sees the mother with a baby on her own, and then the wise men and women, and their entourage come in to save the day. Jack texts – *they chose yours! Nathan's will be used on other media. Where are you?*

The send button is flashing. She didn't press it. He doesn't know. She sends it. It seems forever sitting there.

The nurse comes through the swing door, carrying Ollie. Just an infection she's saying. And Mel realizes. She can only guide him, do her best. There are things we do not know.

And then he's half-standing, stumbling, getting up again, and running towards her.

About the author
Sally Angell has always loved writing. She has won competitions and had short stories in magazines and anthologies. She has run writers groups, and been involved with library activities in Northamptonshire. She likes to explore the truth of emotions and the possibilities of words in her writing.

In the Departure Lounge

Michael Rogers

Betwixt and between. Neither here nor there. Not at home and not away. Between two worlds. One dead. The other powerless to be born. In Limbo. You can't quite relax, because you have to keep an eye open for changes. Change is always threatening. Different flight time. Different gate. Run run run – and when you get there, you're in too much of a hurry to look up properly and see if the plane's going where you're supposed to be going.

Happened to me once at Heathrow. Not that I got on the wrong flight, you understand. That might have been romantic. Sliding Doors. New life. New opportunities. If only I'd. But I didn't. No. Nothing like that. I ran in late. I'd been faffing, looking at things, thinking about buying this, buying that, bargains, calculations, all the idle stuff you do when you're in between with nothing to hang on to, and then I suddenly caught sight of a screen, last call, boarding now, and I hadn't realised before that the gate I had to get to was the furthest away, and airports are BIG, baby. They don't have those little electric cars for no reason, you know, not just because they missed out on Scalextric as kids, no way. In Frankfurt, they have bicycles. Germans are green, you see.

Anyway, I digress. But don't I always, before I get to the place I'm supposed to be going to, before I get to the place that's supposed to be taking me to the place I'm supposed to be going to, while I'm in the departure lounge of the story, on my way to… wherever? Anyway, I rushed into the room and it was empty, empty, empty, and there was a door over the far side and I knew where it led, it led out into that flexy thing, like a giant vacuum hose, all corrugated, that swings out and joins on to the aircraft and

61

I ran down it, too fast, and I slipped up because it was slippery, because it was drizzling outside and the drizzle had blown in and the floor was wet and slimy and I fell down, and the drizzle had come in because there was NOTHING connected to the other end, it was open and empty because the plane had already GONE!!!

That empty feeling in the pit of the stomach you get when some girl dumps you, or you realise you've smashed the rear light of the car you're parking behind, you've done something wrong and it is not, absolutely not, reparable. That's what I had. I tried rationalising, next flight, next day, but then all the elaborate timetable would go to pot, and it *was* elaborate, because I was meeting students of mine that I'd sent all over Germany and Austria as language assistants, travelling by rail, whistlestop, between two trains, a couple of hours chatting in a station buffet (often the best food in town, to tell the truth, that's European culture for you, especially Salzburg, in the old days, but it's all gone now, though they saved the marble and re-erected it in the Augustinian Brewery), and I walked out in deep despair and realised that the flight number on the flipover indicator referred to the NEXT little room, which was still full of people, looking a little impatient by now, because whatever the screen had said to me the flight WASN'T boarding! (Probably waiting for a delivery of halal kosher vegan salami for the in-flight meal.)

So what did I learn from that little escapade? Not to trust signs, unless you know how to interpret them. Be especially wary of switching off your mind. Be on your guard against the mental state you get into in departure lounges. That's what I learnt. But, as with everything you learn, did I remember it? And did I apply it? Listen. Learn.

It was a German airport. Which one? Not Frankfurt, for sure. That's vast. It sprawls. Designed by an algebraic topologist familiar with the problem of the seven Königsberg bridges (don't worry – you *can't* cross all of them only once without repeating yourself – there's a proof, but I've forgotten it, if I ever remembered it, and anyway Königsberg itself was smashed up in the war, and the Russians who took it have never given it back, even though it was the city of Kant, the greatest German philosopher ever, so the Russians certainly wouldn't have bothered about reconstructing it, the way the Poles rebuilt Warsaw from Canaletto's pictures) – Frankfurt is all nodes and ways on that you have to retrace. No shortcuts. The diagram makes it look like a four-leafed clover, for what that's worth.

I think it was Stuttgart. Ought to be a major hub, but isn't. But what a design! That roof! Not unlike King's College Chapel re-imagined in struts and corrugated aluminium. Crossed with a yurt and a one-sided mediaeval knight's pavilion. It rises to a point, but never comes down again on the other side. If only life could be like that! But then I suppose you'd have to die at the climax. Why am I chary of that? Because I like to hope there might be another, even greater climax to come afterwards? Or because I want to savour the decline? Or because I'm just windy?

Stuttgart. And it was deserted. But beautiful. Maybe the one makes up for the other. A trouble shared is a trouble halved. A pleasure shared is a pleasure doubled. But sometimes you think: I appreciate this, but nobody else will. So I'm glad they're not here to spoil my enjoyment.

Nobody selling Glühwein. Probably just as well. All the alcohol evaporates when it sits all day in stainless steel pots, and the wine itself isn't great to start with. No Lebkuchen. No Plätzchen – those little star-shaped almond biscuits you eat every day in Advent, when you light the candle in the middle of the Advent wreath and sit around and think

Christmassy thoughts. None of those horrid little Krampus-figures made out of the shells of some nut or other, possibly the tackiest element of the German Christmas Market. But there was a tree.

(Did I mention it was Christmas? No. I just took it for granted, somehow. But it's important to know. It'll help you understand.)

The tree competed with the roof, and came a creditable second. If it had come first, they wouldn't have been able to fit it in, of course, or it would have looked silly, with the last few centimetres doubled over wispily against the corrugated aluminium. It glittered with baubles and tinsel, helped by the multi-angled spotlights on the roof struts that lit everything but never shone in your eyes. Light everywhere – but you could never be quite sure where it was coming from.

There were presents on it, too, and that worried me. Who could they be *for*? Not the workers at the airport, surely? They'd gone home, as far as I could tell, apart from the one who checked me in. Not for the passengers, either. For nobody? For effect? Just so things looked right? What kind of symbolism was that? Empty boxes in gaudy paper – no, let's be fair, it was relatively tasteful, bright but tasteful, this is Germany, after all, not the UK – but empty: the season of giving – a good impression, and nothing else. Bit too true, that. Not an insight to dwell on, in the season of goodwill. Trouble is, I know the original Latin and understand it, and it doesn't say exactly what you think it should.

In the departure lounge. On my way somewhere else. I forget where the plane was coming from. I knew where it was going to: home. Well, one of the London airports. Not a stopover. Just a pick-up. I looked hard, but I couldn't see a screen. I knew the time, though, and there was a big clock, and there was, as with life, only one way out. But I didn't want to go there just yet. I knew it would be cramped and dingy and functional, only just enough space, and I was enjoying the vastness of the hall with its celestial roof, fretted with golden fire… and the solitude and the silence.

Then I noticed them. I'd not seen them come in. Perhaps I was in too much of a reverie. Three men. One trolley. Odd, lumpy luggage. Not your smooth Samsonite, designed for the overhead locker or under the seat. Three pieces. One each? No labels, not to identify the airline, not to identify the owner. And there was a kind of exotic smell with them. No, two different smells, actually, one sickly sweet, one bitter and pungent. Not the sort of thing you expect in Germany, smells.

I didn't hide behind the tree deliberately, you know. It just sort of happened. And I didn't listen. I just sort of heard. Excellent acoustics in all German public buildings. It goes with the territory.

"This time?" said the black one. He was really handsome and shiny, not sweating, just glowing from inside. There were some kind of initiation slashes on his cheeks, well scarred over, youthful indiscretions that guaranteed reliability for the rest of life, and he was dressed like a Nigerian chief, those wonderful stripy robes, rich colours in the best possible combinations, showing up European regal velvet as the monotonous vulgarity of indoor, pasty-faced people when compared to the orange of the sun and the brown of the earth in all their many gradations. And he had one of those round hats that are never too tall and never too flat, but just right.

"Maybe," said the blonde one. Scandinavian, I thought. Blue eyes, like shadows on snow. A pale tan acquired from soaking up every single drop of sun on long, long days. A deliberate tone of voice, replete with self-questioning, like a Swedish accent.

"One time," said the third. "Sometime." He was shorter than the other two. Swarthy. Dark brown eyes. A chin with stubble, but not quite a beard. "Why don't we ever try – ?"

"My part of the world?" said the African, swirling his robe, that hung over his arm like the drape of a toga.

"We did," said the Swede. "The ones there always have guns."

"Which you make and sell to them."

"My part of the world," said the swarthy one. "Or the New World, for that matter."

"They have guns, too," said the Swede.

"Which they wrest from their oppressors, in the tireless struggle to—"

"Oppress somebody else," said the African, resettling his hat, as if he wasn't quite happy with it.

"You know," said the Swede, "the first one really seemed quite acceptable—"

"In himself he was," said the African, "but—"

"The followers," said the swarthy one, and they all looked at each other and sighed.

"We could always ask the locals," said the Swede.

"Not a good idea," said the African. "Remember what happened last time we tried it?"

Suddenly my mind was filled with an image from Breughel. Blood on snow. Not from a Christmas card. Not *The Return of the Hunters.*

"What do the signs say?" asked the swarthy one.

"Ah," said the Swede, "the signs—"

The African lifted his head to the sky, or rather the roof. Light everywhere – but you could never be quite sure where it was coming from. Then he brought his gaze back down and swept it around the room.

"The signs say – no smoking!"

All three of them laughed heartily with the relief of

66

broken tension. But then the African spotted something else. I couldn't see what it was, because I was on the right of the tree, and partly behind it, and what he was pointing at was on the tree's left. But it must have impressed them all, because they exchanged glances in a highly meaningful way, and their eyes got a light in them that hadn't been there before, and their faces were lit by smiles of anticipation and excitement, and the swarthy one grabbed the trolley and started pushing it in the indicated direction, and because it was a German trolley, that was exactly where it went, and it went so fast and so smoothly that by the time I'd cautiously circled round the tree there was no sign of them at all.

Where had they gone? One wall was entirely glass, reflecting the tree and the baubles till you got dizzy. One wall had the door in it that I'd come through, and the doors to the toilets signed clearly in the international equivalent of Chinese ideograms (toilets for people in skirts, thus including caber tossers and ceremonial Greek guards; and toilets for people in trousers, i.e. everybody else). The third wall contained the exit to the flight gate [I had a feeling there was really only one] and the fourth was taken up by the tree, which was pretty broad at its base.

I looked and looked, and then I saw it. A door of ordinary proportions, plain, well-carpentered wood, with a sturdy frame, and chalked on the lintel a common inscription in German-speaking lands at that time of year: 19 + C + M + B + 96 (though I may have got the last pair of figures wrong – it was a while ago). It looked to me like a cleaner's cupboard, to be honest – somewhere to stack the dustpans and brushes and mops and buckets. But it did have the only lintel within human reach, and the Swabians are pretty strong on scrubbing and sweeping, so any well-appointed airport would have to have such a place.

Should I have... I mean, I did actually put a hand on the handle, but it didn't seem to want to... and then there was an enormous tick of the clock, and I spun round, and it said half-past, and panic seized me (and you will understand why) and I raced through the door in the other wall, and the flight was just boarding, at just the right time, because this *was* Germany after all, and I caught it, and had a nice quarter litre bottle of white Württemberger (Obertürkheimer would have been perfect, but it wasn't, though it was very presentable) and got home in time for Christmas. People usually prefer to go where they know they're going, rather than... Don't you think?

But Christmas doesn't last, does it? And nowadays we tend to ignore what comes after it: those people who arrived too late for the angels, whatever the pictures tell you – not all artists are as reliable as Canaletto (the shepherds had gone by then, too, since sheep can't look after themselves forever). I read a story once about a fourth one, who turned up thirty-three years too late, and found... well, I expect you can imagine what he found.

There's a special word for it, of course, a Greek word, and I fancy myself at Greek etymology, *epiphany*. In all the other Greek words I know, *epi* means *after* or *outside*, like epidermis, and an epitaph is written on the grave or after the burial and an epigram is written *on* something... But I gather that an epiphany is an *appearance*, as in "positively the last..." of somebody famous, and critics of Proust and Joyce use the term for those amazing experiences great writers have (rot them!), that remain forever in the memory and pop up repeatedly in extremely lengthy prose works [come on, this is quite a short one!] like the first time Proust tasted a *madeleine* or the first time he sat on the toilet without the seat down by mistake.

I think I'd rather stick to an English term, though, take

Shakespeare for my model, and call it: *Twelfth Night; or, What You Will.*

But sometimes I really do think about them. Travelling hopefully. Never arriving. Just like the rest of us, in fact; all stuck in the departure lounge, waiting for our flight to be called – but very reluctant to leave just yet.

About the author
Michael has been writing stories since he was eight, and telling (folktales, myths, some original stories) since 2002. He also writes poems, mostly sonnets, which are now appearing in online magazines. He is a Germanist by profession (retired).

Island Views

Margaret Bulleyment

Anna squinted towards the horizon, where distant boats were busily pursuing their maritime business. A hundred miles to… Fecamp, perhaps? What did it matter now?

It was bliss to feel the morning sun on her face. Sophie might have instructed her not to venture out on to the balcony, without her direct supervision, but Anna had no intention of missing a single moment of such a glorious morning.

Paul would have loved this sea view, she thought, as she gingerly lowered herself on to the cushioned chair and would not have cared how many miles away, anywhere was. How content he would have been, to be back in his childhood homeland – but with much better views. If only he could have lasted, just a few more months…

The phone rang and she slowly made her way back into the apartment and picked it up. It could only be Sophie.

"Mum? If you used your mobile, you wouldn't have to get up and walk to the phone every time."

"I need to keep on the move, Sophie. I shall be walking properly again soon and there are new coastal paths to explore here."

"Don't let's get ahead of ourselves," replied Sophie. "Look, I'm not sure what time I'll be with you today. Katy's Ukrainians are arriving this morning, so I'll be round there, helping her settle them in, but I know you'll want to empty the last of the boxes as soon as possible and get your shell collection installed."

"Please thank Graham for putting up my shelves. Once I've got that final box emptied, I shall feel at home. It's a beautiful apartment and I'm really grateful you found it for… u-h… me."

"You can thank Katy for that. She told me her aunt was putting a sea view apartment on the market, when I first approached her about hosting Ukrainians."

"Perhaps I can help Katy with something, in return," Anna suggested. "Please don't worry about my shell box. It's not going anywhere. Katy needs you more than I do, at the moment."

"Let's get you completely mobile before we do anything, shall we? I'll see you later. From what Katy said, you can probably see us all from the back bedroom window. Her new guests should have reached Ryde by now, so we're expecting them in half an hour, or so."

"I'll look out for them, from my watch tower."

That's all I'm good for these days, Anna thought – sitting and watching. Now I'm watching for "them" – "the Ukrainians". Don't they have names? Every day, the television news gets more dreadful, but to turn it off and ignore what is happening to those poor souls, would be a crime.

From the comfort of her bedroom chair, Anna could look down on the avenue below, where both Sophie and Katy lived. Katy's front driveway was almost directly below Anna's apartment.

She nearly missed the anticipated arrival, but jerked awake just in time to see a white taxi sweep up.

The female driver stepped out and helped a very large pregnant woman struggle from the back seat, while from the other side, a young girl slowly emerged, clutching a large woolly dog.

Even from that distance, Anna could see the woman was absolutely exhausted. The girl just stood completely still in the middle of the drive, until Katy and Sophie emerged from the front door and grabbing their guests' battered baggage, ushered them inside.

It was late afternoon by the time Sophie reached Anna and they had settled down together on the balcony, with tea and cake.

"According to *Ukraine Welcome*, the mother is called Anastasia and the girl is Viktoriya," reported Sophie. "Viktoriya's ten. Her dad, Alexander is somewhere on the frontline. Anastasia is constantly scrolling through her phone, trying not to cry and Viktoriya just sits very still, clutching her dog. The dog's called Sasha. They're from somewhere unpronounceable, in southern Ukraine. God knows how long they've been travelling. Katy says that where they lived is more than a thousand miles, just from the Polish border." Sophie paused. "Are you okay with all of this, Mum?"

"Of course, I am. I saw them arrive. When's Anastasia's baby due?"

"I'm not sure. No one told Katy that Anastasia was pregnant, so she's been back in touch with *Ukraine Welcome,* to sort out baby supplies. If the worst comes to the worst, Katy's daughter might still have a few baby things tucked away in her loft.

"Anastasia speaks a few words of English and we do a bit of translation using the phone, but Viktoriya has not uttered a single word and barely eaten anything either. I don't know why."

"You don't know why?" exclaimed Anna.

"What do you mean, Mum?"

"Her family has been bombed out of its home. She and her mother have travelled two thousand miles, across Europe – the first thousand in their own country, torn by war. They have left everything behind to reach another country, whose language they don't speak and whose alphabet they don't recognise, to live with complete strangers, while their husband and father is somewhere unknown, risking his life. Oh… and they are about to increase the family."

Anna paused for breath. "What do you expect them to do – talk about the weather?"

"I know it's difficult for you, Mum," said Sophie, standing up abruptly. "So shall we just get these shells out of their box and on to your beautiful new glass shelves?"

Two days later, Anna woke to the sound of an ambulance siren, followed by the phone ringing.

"Mum? Sorry to wake you, but we have a crisis. Anastasia has been taken away in the ambulance – possible premature labour – and Katy has gone with her. I'm here in Katy's house to look after Viktoriya, so I won't be round to you, until that's all sorted."

Anna saw no point in returning to bed, so she dressed and took her breakfast out on to the balcony. The sun has just risen on another beautiful day, but how beautiful depends on who you are, where you are and who is with you.

Paul would have scoffed at a beautiful sunrise, but he would have been out in the garden, as soon as he could, watering before it got too hot, weeding and pruning. As lovely as the sea view was, Anna was missing her garden bursting with Paul's favourites – red and gold salvias and marigolds; pink and purple fuchsias and cool, green ferns.

The phone rang again.

"Mum? Viktoriya's gone missing! We were looking for Anastasia's phone, but while I was making breakfast, Viktoriya found it and just disappeared, taking it with her. I've hunted through the house and garden, I've phoned home to Graham, who is calling the police and we're both going to drive round looking for her. She could be anywhere. Why would she run off like that?"

"For the same reasons, I've already told you," sighed

Anna. "I am going out." She hunted around for her stick and then a step at a time, headed for the lift. From the entrance hall, it was only a few yards to the gate, which took her out into the community garden. The seat with the best view, beside a magnificent red phormium, was already occupied by a young girl, clutching a large woolly dog and scrolling through a phone. Anna approached gently.

"May I sit here, too?" she asked. "I can't walk any further."

The child looked at her blankly and then down at the phone. There were tears in her eyes.

"Everything will be all right," said Anna, sitting down beside her. "Trust me."

She took a very deep breath. She had to do this.

"*Ya mogu ponyat tebya… po russki* – 'I can understand you… in Russian?' *Ya Anna* – 'I'm Anna.' *Ya pol'ka* – 'I'm Polish'."

She pointed at the child. "*Vy Viktoriya?* – 'You are Viktoriya?'" Then she pointed at the dog. "*On Sasha?* – 'He is Sasha?'"

Viktoriya looked curiously at Anna, as she continued in Russian. "*You are staying with Katy and you have met my daughter, Sophie.*"

Viktoriya clutched Sasha tightly, twisting his tail in her hand. "*You are Sophie's mother?*" she replied slowly, in Russian.

"*Yes. I live up there and I can see Katy's house, from my bedroom window. I saw you arrive on Tuesday, with your mother. I have just moved here too. I am missing my garden. My husband was our gardener and when he died, I couldn't cope with it anymore. But here, I have a sea view and I'm on an island – what could be better?*

"*It's colder outside today, than I thought and I should have brought a cushion. Would you and Sasha like to come indoors with me, for some hot chocolate and biscuits?*"

Viktoriya nodded slowly and helped Anna up from the seat. They were inside the apartment, before she let go of Anna's arm.

"I'll make the chocolate and then I'll phone Sophie and tell her where you are," said Anna. *"Have a seat."*

When Anna returned, from the kitchen she found Viktoriya sitting on the floor, gazing up at the shells above her.

"These are so beautiful," said Viktoriya. *"Where did you get them?"*

Anna smiled, put the tray on the coffee table and sat down on the sofa.

"My shells come from coasts and islands all over the world. When I was your age, I'd never seen the sea. Poland's coastline is in the north, but we lived much further south, in a village, in the forest. My father was a forester. Not like in a fairy story with an axe over his shoulder, but in a proper uniform."

"My Papa is fighting for Ukraine in the war, but he's in trouble," Viktoriya said, quietly. *"I am finding it difficult to understand what is happening and my mother got some messages that made her very upset. He is in hiding, as the Russians are saying he is a Ukrainian spy.*

"Papa has a Russian mother and a Ukrainian father and was born in Russia, but has lived in Ukraine, since he was a tiny baby. Mumiya is Ukrainian too. I'm very worried and I don't know what to do and now my mother's ill too… What if she dies? What will happen to me?"

Viktoriya jumped up, tears running down her cheeks and darted across to Anna, who reached out and pulling her down on to the sofa, wrapped her arms tightly around her. *"You will be safe, Viktoriya, I promise you. You will be safe here."*

Anna held Viktoriya, closer and closer, until she had stopped crying.

"This is my family," Viktoriya said suddenly, unzipping Sasha and pulling out a photo. *"Here we all are last summer, having a picnic in the garden. It seems such a long, long, time ago. There's Mumiya and Papa and those are my grandparents... They're both dead now."*

"Your Papa's called Sasha, isn't he? said Anna quickly, pointing at the smiling young man in the photo, with his arm round Viktoriya, *"...short for Aleksander?"*

"Yes," muttered Viktoriya, burying her face between the dog's huge paws.

"Would you like to sit out on the balcony, Viktoriya?" said Anna. *"There's a lovely view and I must phone Sophie and tell her where you are."*

"Sophie? Listen… I found Viktoriya in the community garden and she's here with me," said Anna, rapidly. "It's a long story, but she's safe. There's no need to come rushing over here, we are enjoying some hot chocolate."

"What? I'm coming straight away. Anastasia's fine. She's not in labour yet, but they are keeping her in the hospital, so I will come and collect Viktoriya, take her to see her mother and then I can bring Katy back too."

"Good news," said Anna, joining Viktoriya and Sasha on the balcony. *"Your mother's fine and Sophie is taking you to see her. Would you like to come and look at my shells, while we wait?"*

"I'd like that."

Anna lifted a large shell from the top shelf and carefully handed it down to Viktoriya. *"This one's a conch, from the Seychelles."*

Viktoriya gently slipped her fingers inside the pearly, pink lip of the shell. *"It's so heavy, but so smooth and warm and beautiful."* Her thumb stroked the thick piecrust edge. *"…And strong."*

She needed two hands, to turn it over and over and round and round. *"The spikes look like a submarine coming towards you, this way, but when I tip it up, with the spikes on top, it's like a... temple?... somewhere."*

"Thailand, perhaps?" suggested Anna. *"I thought the same."*

They shared a brief moment of quiet, before the front door flew open and Sophie burst in. "Viktoriya, don't do that ever again. I was so worried about you. You must never run off like that."

"That's enough, Sophie," said Anna, stepping in. "This is not the time and place. Viktoriya and I have had a long conversation and I will tell you all about it later."

"A long conversation?" Sophie looked incredulous. "How on earth, did you manage...? You didn't...?"

"I did," said Anna emphatically, "and I'm still here to tell the tale. Off you go with Viktoriya and please bring her back tomorrow. She won't start school until Monday, will she?"

"No, but..."

"That's fine, then."

Anna turned to Viktoriya. *"I'll see you tomorrow. Is that all right? We can put the last of the shells in place and perhaps we could make some pierogi."*

"I would like that, Baba Anna."

Sasha waved a paw and Viktoriya followed Sophie, out of the door.

It was evening before Anna phoned Sophie and tried to explain what Viktoriya had told her.

Sophie's questions came in a torrent. "Her father's a Ukrainian spy, Mum? Is that true? Could he be a Russian one? Are they the other side? What do we actually know about them? Is Russian her first language?"

"For pity's sake, grow up, Sophie. Everything is not black and white. Half of Ukraine speaks Russian. Viktoriya and her family speak Ukrainian and Russian."

"And you're speaking it! You haven't told Viktoriya…"

"No. Trust me, Sophie. Viktoriya's just a girl who's missing her family. I listened and made her smile and that's all that matters. I'll see you tomorrow – although Viktoriya could walk here by herself, it's only up the road."

"Absolutely not."

Sophie arrived with Viktoriya and Sasha, the next morning. "I can't stop, Mum," Sophie said, already backing to the door, "Anastasia's finally gone into labour, so Katy's heading to the hospital, I'm off to collect the rest of the baby equipment and I'll see you and Viktoriya later."

"That's exciting news, Viktoriya," said Anna. "Do you know whether it will be a boy, or a girl?"

"No. Mum didn't want to know," replied Viktoriya. "Baba Anna? Is Sophie your only child?"

"Yes."

"Do you have any grandchildren?"

"No, Sophie and Graham didn't have any children. You call me Baba Anna, so perhaps I am your Polish/English grandmother."

"I call you that, because that's what I want you to be."

"I'm old enough to be your great-grandmother," laughed Anna. "Let's finish the shells, shall we?"

Anna gently lifted each shell out of its wrappings and let Viktoriya decide where to put it.

"Oh, these stripey ones are pretty, Baba Anna. They should go in the middle. They look like clowns."

"Looks can be deceptive. They are cone shells – corni magi – magicians' hats – and they can kill."

"Magicians' hats? Clowns and hats. It's a circus! They don't kill people, do they?"

"Well, I don't think they lie in wait on the Great Barrier Reef for a sunburnt tourist to come swimming past, but if you trod on one, you would be squirted with a lethal liquid, for which there is no antidote."

"Wow! Scary clowns, then. What about these, Baba?"

"Those are cowries and scallops. They are quite humble shells, but they have a place – like all shells, they have been someone's home."

"I've never thought of shells, as homes, Baba."

"That's what they are and when one creature has finished with its home, it becomes someone else's home. Do you know what a hermit crab is?"

"I've heard of them, but…"

"They don't have a shell – a home, of their own. They just go round finding ones, that others have left behind. As the crab grows, it needs a larger shell – a different home. We're like hermit crabs. We go from place to place with new shells, then we grow out of them and move on, leaving traces behind for others.

"I like that idea, Baba."

"I'm glad. Do you also like music, Viktoriya? Graham, my son-in-law, has set up my CD player and I can hear wonderful music again. He wants me to have some new gadget, but I'm happy with what I have." Anna sorted through a pile of CDs. *"Ah, Prokofiev. Perfect. Ukraine's finest."*

"Romeo and Juliet," said Viktoria, recognising it and jumping up, to conduct. *"Papa loves his music."*

"I do too, Viktoriya. Music expresses what cannot be captured in words – and best of all, needs no translation."

Viktoria stopped conducting. *"Can I ask you something, Baba Anna?"*

"Of course, you can."

"Why don't you like speaking Russian? I don't like it either but…"

"How did...?"

"You speak it well, it's old-fashioned, but..."

"You're a very wise young lady, Viktoriya, but it's a long story and long stories call for hot chocolate. See you on the balcony, in a few minutes."

"I can do it, Baba," said Viktoriya, dancing into the kitchen. *"You sit down. I will bring it to you. You can look after Sasha."*

Anna was gazing out at the sea, Sasha on her lap, when Viktoriya returned with the tray.

"I think I have everything," she said, handing Anna her chocolate, *"so I'm all ready for your story."*

Anna sat Sasha on her knee. *"I was four, when soldiers burst into our forest home one night and told us to be ready to leave in thirty minutes. They didn't tell us where we were going. I was too young to know that Germany and Russia had invaded Poland and divided it between them and that Polish deportations happened regularly. Nor did I know, why we had to leave. I just know that my parents, my younger brother and I, were loaded on to overcrowded cattle trucks in appalling conditions and those of us who survived the journey, emerged days and days later, at a camp in Siberia."*

Viktoriya put her chocolate down, went to reach for Sasha, but changed her mind.

"I have never been so cold, before, or since," Anna continued. *"We were poorly fed and everyone, had to work. The children collected wood in the forest and it wasn't a fairytale. I won't describe the conditions to you, but my little brother died very quickly and my father, just a few weeks later. He was called Sasza, like your father... My mother was a nurse and fought for our survival. I have no idea what she did, but eventually, we arrived back in Poland.*

"The war was over, but the nightmare had not ended. Our own Polish people called us Sybiraks – the Siberian exiles. At school, they used to shout it, while they punched me. There was suspicion about us. Were we enemies of the people? Even today, I don't fully understand, why it was us. My father was the leader of the foresters in our area. Was that it? What danger was that to them? Why did they take our whole family? Or was it all just an elaborate excuse to move two million people, to show the other millions what could happen to them?

"Gradually, my dear resourceful mother managed to move us from Poland to East Germany and then one day, I fell asleep and woke up feeling very strange... in West Germany. I never did ask her what she had done to get us out. Then we moved on to the Netherlands and there I saw the sea – for the very first time.

"Mother was determined to get to Britain, or as she correctly called it, the British Isles – all of it, every last little island. The Red Cross helped us. Mother had a relative whose husband was in the Polish Air Force and had been stationed in England, during the war. He had helped keep the country safe, so now my mother wanted the British Isles to keep the two of us, safe.

"She said, 'Anna, islands are safe havens. They are surrounded by water. Invaders can only cross in boats, or by plane and if they fail, they drown in the sea. The sea and only the sea, is the boundary. No ugly soldiers, carrying weapons and stamping around in big boots, can just step over a line and attack you.'

"I have inherited her love of islands and I have spent more than seventy years, living on this one. Paul and I travelled to many distant, warmer islands, but we kept exploring our island home – especially the coastal path. It goes round the whole of Great Britain and if you keep

81

walking – for nearly three thousand miles – you will be back where you started from. All that way and you are still in the same safe country, with the same view of the sea. You and the island will have changed a little, but you have come back home – returned to your starting point – just a little wiser.

"Now I'm on the final miles of my life, I'm on a smaller island – it's only seventy miles all the way around the Isle of Wight. My husband was born here, but on a council estate, with no view. He wanted to come back to where he had started from, but with better views. Sadly, he died before we could move here. So, I'm here – but in a smaller shell.

"I vowed, when I was your age and we had left Siberia, that no Russian word would ever pass my lips again. It never did until…"

"…you met me, Baba Anna."

"Yes, and when I didn't speak Ukrainian, all that mattered was you… Your chocolate's getting cold, Viktoriya."

Viktoriya picked up her mug.

"So, a clever girl like you, does speak English?"

"Yes. Back home I am top of the class for English, but I cannot think, or speak, about my family, in English – it doesn't… sound real… or true… or right."

"I understand that, Viktoriya, I really do, but one day it will and never forget, English is the richest language in the world – all because of the invaders, the refugees and the immigrants who did make it across the water, bringing their language and customs which centuries later, are all part of this nation's rich heritage." Anna laughed. "I still sound like a teacher."

"Baba? Was your mother still living when the Channel Tunnel opened?"

"No, she wasn't, but I think she wouldn't have minded. Crossing under the sea, sounds even more difficult, than crossing over it.

"Now young lady," she continued, "As school starts on Monday, perhaps it's time we spoke English all the time. I taught for thirty-five years – Geography."

"That's not a surprise for me," laughed Viktoriya. She paused.

"Baba. The cone shells… are they evil because they try to kill people who step on their homes?"

"What do you mean? They are just creatures that do what they have to do, instinctively."

"But if someone steps on your home, you fight back, don't you? Even if that means killing someone. The Russians have stepped on us, haven't they and we are fighting back. Papa has…"

"We all do what we have to in order to survive, Viktoriya, so we must not think that…"

The phone rang, cutting short Anna's reply.

"Why don't you answer, Viktoriya, while I bring everything in from outside. It might be news of your mother."

"Hello, this is Viktoriya speaking. Yes… Baba Anna is fine. She asks me to answer the phone in English… Aah, that's wonderful news, thank you, Sophie, thank you, thank you.

"I have a beautiful baby sister, Baba."

"That's exciting news, Viktoriya," called Anna, from the kitchen. "We must celebrate. I have some fizzy lemonade, somewhere in this fridge."

"But first I must talk to Papa's friend. He sends us news of Papa." Viktoriya quickly unzipped Sasha, and pulled out the phone.

"Don't expect too much," Anna cautioned.

"It's fine, I think… Yes! Yes! Yes! Yes! Yes!" Viktoriya danced up and down, the phone still stuck to her ear. "They've got Papa out and he's in Poland!"

"Three cheers for my native land!" screamed Anna.

Viktoriya was dancing around, punching the air. "They will give him news of his new daughter! Victory for Viktoriya! Victory for Ukraine! Yeah! Yeah! Yeah!"

"Come and sit out here with your lemonade, Victory Girl."

"Sophie is coming soon, Baba, to take me to see Mumiya and Margita."

"Margita?"

"The name for a girl was Margita and for a boy, Pavlo."

"You know that Margita, means a pearl, don't you?"

"I like that, Baba. Pink, pearly and strong, like the conch."

"It looks like your family is moving on to a larger shell now, Viktoriya. Let's raise our glasses to that. Na zdrowie, Viktoriya!"

"Budmo, Baba Anna!"

"Cheers to us both!"

About the author

Margaret Bulleyment, a retired teacher from Oxfordshire, has had short stories published on story websites and in anthologies, including Bridge House's *Baubles*; *Glit-er-ary*; *Crackers*, *Nativity* and *Evergreen*, and was awarded second prize in the Daphne du Maurier Short Story Competition 2022, judged by Raynor Winn.

She has had short plays performed professionally, as an Ovation Theatre Awards finalist and her children's play *Caribbean Calypso* was runner-up in Trinity College of Music and Drama's 2011 International Playwriting Competition. It has been performed three times in Bangalore, by educational charity Jagriti Kids.

She enjoys choral singing and gardening, but fortunately for her neighbours, not at the same time.

Margaret is dedicating this story to her granddaughter Francesca, who also loves writing stories.

Lavender

Sara Winslow

At precisely 9:17 each night, the rumbling of the Lavender Express along the railroad tracks roused Evelyn from the davenport. After easing the creakiness out of her knees, she would take Daisy in the backyard for her last tinkle of the day. Evelyn always felt a thrill seeing the night sky shine light purple, mixing her two favourite colours (pale pink and sky blue). After the glow subsided and they went back inside the cosy bungalow, the little white terrier would trot to the bedroom and curl up on Evelyn's pillow. Evelyn would wash the supper dishes, letting the water soak warmth into her hands. Then she'd do her own tinkle and brush her teeth.

Each night in the lavatory mirror, Evelyn acknowledged the old lady gazing back at her. Hair silvering, face splotching, creasing, sagging. Still-dark eyebrows simultaneously thinning and sprouting cowlicks. Eyes being crowded by bags above and below. The fetching girl who had once looked back at her with anticipation was nowhere to be found. Each night, Evelyn asked the woman in the mirror, "What is the measure of a life? Is it how many wrinkles, how many silver hairs? Is it the career I had, the Michelin star, the recipes I created, the meals I cooked? The relationships? The break-ups? The regrets I've carried? The ones I've let go?" The old lady would simply stare back at her, mimicking her words, providing no answers.

Once finished with the mirror, Evelyn would change into her pale pink flannel pajamas, retrieve the key hidden under her mattress, unlock the nightstand drawer, check that Aunt Lillian's ring was safely in its box, re-lock the drawer, and re-hide the key. Finally, Evelyn would scoot

Daisy over, tuck herself beneath the pink and blue patchwork quilt, and close her eyes.

Every night went just like this, until one Saturday in November, when Daisy jumped off the davenport and began pacing by the back door. The film Evelyn was watching had ended, her glass of claret drained, her eyelids heavy. But the Lavender Express hadn't rumbled by.

"Settle down, girl. It's not time yet."

Daisy whined. Evelyn looked at the grandmother clock. 9:45! Where in the world was the Lavender Express? She strained to remember where the emergency lantern might be, then found it in the milk cupboard just inside the back door, where she kept such things. Evelyn held the lantern high as she and Daisy carefully stepped into the Lavenderless night.

The air smelled of the winter that was coming. A sharp wind blew open Evelyn's fuzzy sky-blue sweater. She wrapped its warmth back around herself. Daisy growled, a slow, gravelly one unfamiliar to Evelyn. She shone the lantern in the direction of the growl. Daisy crouched by the garden shed, ears pulled back, lip arranged in a snarl, tail held low.

"Who's there?" Evelyn shouted, hoping the trembling in her voice didn't show. No one answered. Daisy continued to growl.

"Who's there?" Evelyn shouted once more. "I have a weapon. I'll call the police."

Silence.

"I'm getting ready to shoot! Three… two…"

The door swung open, revealing a South Asian-looking man, lean and sinewy, with the most beautiful face. He exited the shed, hands held high. "Don't shoot," he pleaded.

Daisy's growl turned into excited little barks. Her ears relaxed, her lip uncurled, her tail lifted. She approached the stranger, sniffed his feet, tentatively wagged.

"May I?" the stranger asked Evelyn. "May I pat your pooch?"

"Very well," she responded. "Just keep your hands where I can see them." She was still pretending she had a weapon, though the lantern was obviously all she held.

The stranger squatted down and offered his hand to Daisy, who began to lick it with great interest. Evelyn saw that it was bleeding.

"You're hurt," she said.

"Only a scratch," the stranger replied. "I'm – I'm sorry I trespassed into your shed. The Lavender Express broke down. I was looking for a place to spend the night."

"You were on the Lavender Express? It broke down?"

The man nodded.

"Well, that explains quite a lot," Evelyn said. She didn't like interruptions to her nighttime routine, but here was a wounded man. "Sit at the patio table," she directed him. "I'll get something to clean up that hand."

Evelyn went inside to find the first aid kit. On her way back out, she grabbed the pepper spray from the back-door cupboard and tucked it in her pocket, just in case.

"I'm Mark," the man declared once Evelyn returned. "Mark Chatterjee."

"Evelyn. And that's Daisy. Now set your hand on the table. This might sting." The lantern light was low and Evelyn hadn't thought to wear her glasses, but she cleaned Mark's wound as best she could. It was rather more than a scratch. She fumbled in the first aid kit for a gauze bandage. The wind snatched the gauze from her fingers, swollen with age and no longer nimble. The bandage whooshed to the ground.

"Drat!" Evelyn exclaimed. She couldn't possibly use dirty gauze on a clean wound. Her arthritic fingers went back for another bandage. Again the wind blew, again she lost it. This wouldn't do. It would be unwise to invite this stranger into her home, though, wouldn't it? She looked down at Daisy, trustingly snuggled between Mark's foot and his sand-colored canvas knapsack. Daisy had always been a good judge of character. "We'd better go inside," Evelyn said, patting her pocket to make sure the pepper spray was still there.

Inside, Evelyn parked her visitor at the kitchen table, where the bandaging took far less effort.

"How did this happen?"

Mark looked at his hand. "Thank you for taking care of it. I'm embarrassed to say I tumbled off the top of the Lavender Express when it broke down."

"You were riding on top of the Lavender Express?"

"Well, I, umm, didn't have a ticket. I'm sorry."

"There's no shame in being poor," Evelyn told him, while considering whether he was setting her up to ask for money. Out loud, she said, "It's a good thing you weren't hurt any worse. Were you headed home? Or leaving home?"

"Neither, exactly. I've been staying with friends in Fieldtown. I grew up in St. Petunia. I go back to visit my mom's grave." He visibly swallowed.

Evelyn examined Mark's face. His eyes looked steadily back at hers. He seemed to be speaking the truth. Part of Evelyn worried about his intentions and wanted to get him out of her house. But another part of her recognized that here was a young man in need. With her nighttime routine already disrupted beyond repair, what was a smidge more trouble? She pressed down on the table to lift herself out of the chair, and set a hand on his shoulder. "You'll stay on the davenport tonight," she said, then instantly regretted her generosity. She got him settled on the davenport anyway.

After getting ready for bed, she locked herself and

Daisy in the bedroom, wedged a chair under the knob, and set the pepper spray on her nightstand.

Sunday morning, Evelyn woke to the smell of coffee and flapjacks. The visitor, the one she had recklessly allowed to stay – he was using her kitchen! She glanced at the chair, still jammed under the doorknob. Just to be sure, she got the key from under the mattress, unlocked the nightstand drawer, found the little box in back, opened it up. The ring was there, thank heavens, just as it had been the night before. She ran her fingertip across the cool stone. A rare lavender diamond, four carats, emerald cut. Left by her Aunt Lillian, who had lived past her ninety-third birthday, too late in Evelyn's life for the ring to be of use. Evelyn would never wear it and would never want to sell it. What would she do with all that money? Aunt Lillian always claimed the ring had some sort of magical power, but of course that was nonsense. So the diamond stayed in Evelyn's nightstand. Perhaps she should squirrel it away in a safe deposit box, but it comforted her to have the ring nearby, a reminder of her beloved aunt in all her deluded extravagance.

Now, relieved that the diamond hadn't been pilfered, Evelyn placed it back in the drawer, locked it up, hid the key. She pulled on her fluffy white robe, slid the pepper spray into a pocket, unwedged the chair from under the doorknob, and hurried to the kitchen. There stood Mark, cooking flapjacks at the stove with his bandaged hand. Daisy, tail wagging furiously, scampered over to him.

"Good morning, Daisy. Good morning, Evelyn. I hope you don't mind, I'm making us breakfast. Your kitchen is amazing." Before Evelyn decided whether to explain that she had a wall knocked down years ago to expand the kitchen into her childhood bedroom, he continued: "You didn't have eggs, so I used baking powder instead. I think they're coming out great." He tipped the skillet toward her.

They did look pretty great. Not everyone knew how to make vegan flapjacks. But what cheek this young man had! Shouldn't he be going on his way, not dirtying up her kitchen?

"I must say, Mark, I didn't expect you to stay for breakfast." Evelyn's own coldness startled her. It was necessary, though. She didn't want to be taken advantage of. She'd already been foolish enough.

"I'm sorry. How about I stay long enough to serve you, then I'll go?"

"Very well," Evelyn replied. A person who made such lovely flapjacks clearly wasn't planning to rob or otherwise harm her, was he? She let Daisy outside and headed to the lavatory.

A few minutes later, Evelyn made her way to the breakfast table, which Mark had set with a plate of golden flapjacks, a mug of steaming coffee, and a tiny bouquet of late-season pansies from the back yard. "Very nice indeed," Evelyn murmured after her first bite of maple syrup-soaked goodness. Perhaps she had been too hasty sending him away. "Why don't you stay for breakfast," she offered. "We wouldn't want to waste all these flapjacks."

After setting another place and sitting at it, Mark announced, "They said on the radio that the Lavender Express will be running again this evening."

He listened to her radio? This young man was certainly making himself at home! "I'm wondering, Mark, how do you find yourself without the resources to buy a train ticket or a hotel room?"

Mark took a few swallows of coffee before answering. "I didn't plan to end up broke."

"As I said last night, there's no shame in being poor. Life has been decent to me, financially I mean. But I know it could have been otherwise." Evelyn silently chastised herself for mentioning her financial status. What if he was one of those swindlers they always warned about? No, no, Mark couldn't be one of those. She even detected some nutmeg in the flapjacks and cinnamon in the coffee.

"Good luck telling my father there's no shame being poor," Mark replied, shaking his head. "The reason I have no money – I have this dream to run a place with an open mic where people can come and play music or do stand-up. Share their poetry. A coffeehouse during the day and a wine bar at night. A community center, really."

"Sounds wonderful."

"Thank you. I opened it in Fieldtown. Called it Prema, after my mom." Mark stared into his coffee.

"How lovely," Evelyn said.

Mark looked up. "It was lovely. But it didn't do well. I had to close it down, couldn't make the rent. Pitiful."

"Don't say pitiful. You were following your dream."

"I was. Now I've got a day job, but I'm living in my friends' basement and saving up to try again."

"So that's why you didn't buy a ticket for the Lavender Express?"

Mark nodded. "I think my idea will work better in a bigger town. I'm putting away all my earnings to move to the city so I can open Prema there."

Evelyn wondered anew whether Mark aimed to get money from her. Perhaps not to swindle her, but to convince her to invest. Did he know who she was? "You could have bought a cheap seat on the commuter train," she cajoled. "It's only a few dollars."

"I know. But I have to take the Lavender Express." His voice caught. "My mom used to love seeing the night sky light up when it came through St. Petunia. Lavender was her favorite color." Mark looked down into his nearly empty cup.

Could this lavender business be something he invented to gain her sympathy? Evelyn's mind strayed to Aunt Lillian's lavender diamond. Surely he didn't know about that. She reached across the table, patted his good hand. "That makes sense then, Mark. You should be proud of yourself for pursuing your dream."

He looked up. "Thank you, Evelyn, Sometimes I am. My father, though—" Mark stopped, gulped the remainder of his coffee.

"Let me guess. Your father disapproves."

Mark's eyes danced a bit. "You guessed right!"

"My parents didn't approve of my career choice either. They thought I should do something more ladylike." Evelyn didn't tell Mark that her parents disapproved of more than her career choice.

"What did you do?"

"I was a chef. At Flaxen, the fine-dining vegan – I mean plant-based – restaurant in the city." Mark raised his eyebrows. "Don't look at me that way, Mark, female chefs do exist."

"I know. It's just that—" Mark stopped himself, tilted his head slightly.

"Oh, I see. You young people think you invented plant-based. But not everyone in my generation is backward thinking," Evelyn teased.

"Of course. I didn't mean to offend you, Evelyn. And I'm not young, by the way, I'm about to be forty-two!"

The corners of Evelyn's mouth turned up. "You don't realize it now, but forty-two is young. I remember what long hours I could endure in my forties. My dream, you see, was to earn a Michelin star."

"Did you ever get one?"

"Why yes, I did." Evelyn felt that familiar swell of bittersweet pride in her chest.

"Congratulations! I feel a little sheepish, cooking breakfast for such a renowned chef."

"Don't be silly, Mark. Your flapjacks are delectable. I appreciate the nutmeg you sprinkled in." Evelyn took another bite. "I want to tell you something, though." She set her fork down. "It's important to follow your career dreams. But don't lose sight of the rest of your life. I had a wonderful career."

"You did!"

"Yes, but now the only thing I have to show for my life is that Michelin star. Never had any children. My partner left me long ago." Evelyn's hand drifted to the spot behind her left ear where Flora had that one perfect little mole. "My career," she continued, "striving for that star, it didn't mix well with a relationship. That star – I worked so hard for it, I wanted it so much. It's meaningless now." For a moment, Evelyn let herself wonder what Flora was doing now, if she was also alone, whether her bright blonde hair had silvered.

"You don't work as a chef anymore?" Mark asked.

Evelyn shook her head. "I retired years back, moved here to Flowertown."

"Then you have time for a relationship. You could meet someone new. There are plenty of men out there." Evelyn wrinkled her nose. "Or women," Mark hurriedly added. "I didn't mean to presume."

She chuckled. "The only thing I'd need a man for is to change the lightbulbs I can't reach."

Mark sat up a mite straighter. "You need some lightbulbs changed? I can do that before I leave."

Was this offer of help part of a plan to ask her for money? Evelyn didn't want to be a fool. But she really did need some lightbulbs changed. And wasn't it better to trust him, now that she'd already let him into her house? After he'd spent the night, made her a wonderful breakfast? "That would be much appreciated, Mark. The things I used to do slip a little from my reach every day. Getting old isn't fun."

"Maybe not, but like my namesake said, it's a privilege denied to many."

"Your namesake?"

"Mark Twain," he explained. "My parents came here from India. Mom wanted so badly for me to fit in. She wanted to name me something completely American. So that's my name, Mark Twain Chatterjee. You can imagine how well a boy with that name would fit in."

"Oh my, what a name!"

He laughed. "I used to hate it! But I've grown proud of it. I've memorized a lot of sayings from the first Mark Twain. That's what I meant about getting old being a privilege. He said, 'Do not regret growing older. It is a privilege denied to many.'"

"Why, that's one way of looking at it."

"It's the only way I look at it. My mom died when she was forty-one. The same age I am now." Mark's voice wavered. He looked at his plate.

Evelyn's heart panged a smidgen for him. He couldn't possibly be making all this up to trick her; no one could be that skilled of an actor. Even so, when she had him change the lightbulb in the drawing room, she kept it to herself that one in the bedroom also needed changing. She didn't want him too close to Aunt Lillian's ring.

After Mark changed the drawing room lightbulb, fixed a leaky faucet, and carried the rubbish out to the curb, he accompanied Evelyn and Daisy on their midday walk. It was a splendid day, a brilliant blue sky, sun dazzling the lacy branches of the leafless trees. Sweet bungalows populated the neighborhood, painted all sorts of charming colors (Evelyn's was periwinkle).

"It's beautiful here," Mark observed.

"Why yes, it is," Evelyn answered. "Sometimes I forget."

"What made you decide to retire here, instead of staying in the city?"

They stopped so Daisy could give a proper sniff to the trunk of a particularly fascinating tree. Evelyn took a deep breath. "This is where I come from. I never planned to move back. I loved living in the city. Then my father passed, and my mother was alone."

"Oh, I'm sorry."

"Nothing to be sorry about, dear. They lived good, long lives. But Mother declined after Dad passed. She refused to leave home and I didn't have the heart to force her. So I moved back in. It was almost time to retire anyway." Evelyn glanced at her hands. "My arthritis was slowing me down. And those long nights were taking their toll." She chose not to mention the investors who had pressured her to step aside and make room for someone younger, how they made it financially attractive to give up her restaurant.

Daisy, finished with the tree, trotted on. The humans followed, Evelyn continuing her story. It was years in the past, and her parents had lived well into their eighties. Yet, talking about it awakened a dull pain in the vicinity of her heart.

"Mother ended up passing a few years later. Nearly a decade ago now. I could have moved back to the city, but I stayed." Evelyn didn't say how little was left for her in the city once Flora and the restaurant were both gone. "Honestly, I couldn't bear to sell the bungalow," she said instead. "The one my mother refused to leave. It's the house where I grew up. And I suppose now I'm the one who refuses to leave!" Evelyn pressed her lips together. She meant that as a kind of joke, but in truth, she sometimes wondered if she was becoming her mother.

"Makes sense that you'd want to stay. It's a beautiful home. And a beautiful neighborhood."

"Why, thank you. Yes, I suppose I'll die here, too, like Mother." This reminded her, she hadn't drawn up that will she had been meaning to. She planned to leave the bungalow to a worthy organization. Mark couldn't conceivably be after her house, could he? Still, it seemed prudent to tell him that she had already written her will (even if that was a bit of a fib).

"My will leaves the house to the Indian tribe whose ancestral lands these are," she told him, surprised at how easy it was to lie.

"Wow, what an admirable thing to do!"

"Oh, I don't know about that. It would be far more admirable if I gave it back before I died." Evelyn experienced a drop of regret for lying to Mark, but realized this was indeed what she wanted her will to say. "I feel like George Washington, freeing people in his will, while he enslaved them during his life. Besides, I don't even know if the tribe wants the house."

"What's their name?" Mark asked.

"Whose name?"

"The indigenous tribe."

Another quote by the first Mark Twain popped into Evelyn's head: "If you tell the truth, you don't have to remember anything." She managed to say that she couldn't remember the tribe's name offhand, but it was written in her will. She felt ashamed that she didn't know the name. She would look it up first thing tomorrow, and get her will done soon, too.

Mark continued his questions: "It doesn't upset your relatives? That you're not keeping the house in the family?"

Evelyn couldn't tell if he was just making conversation, or if he suspected her dissembling. "I'm not close to my relatives," she said.

"I'm not either," Mark responded, before Evelyn had a chance to consider whether her admission had been wise.

Evelyn felt her belly unclench as she grasped the opportunity to change the subject. "You don't have family left in St. Petunia?"

"Just my father. Everyone else is back in India."

"Well, I'm sure he'll be thrilled to see you!"

Mark turned his eyes to the sidewalk. "We don't talk."

Evelyn remembered the weight of the years she had been estranged from her own parents. "Oh, dear," she said. "Whatever it is, perhaps you can make it up with him. Like that Mark Twain quote you recited – not everyone is privileged enough to grow old. Not everyone is privileged enough to have a parent grow old."

Mark, still looking down, nodded.

"Will you do something for me? Will you go see your dad while you're there?"

Mark raised his eyes. "For you, Evelyn, I will."

"Really?" she teased. "Or are you just saying that to placate me?"

He shrugged.

Evelyn's smile drooped. "Please see your father," she urged. "I didn't speak to mine for years. He didn't approve of me. And by the time my Aunt Lillian convinced me to go see him anyway, he was so far gone he didn't recognize me." Could those be tears stinging the corners of her eyes? Thank goodness for her sunglasses!

"I'll go see him, Evelyn. I really will."

She invited Mark to stay for another meal. He wanted to set out before dark, so they agreed on a late lunch/early supper. Mark chopped onions and sliced mushrooms while Evelyn sautéed and stirred the ingredients into a risotto. She recalled the days when she had help in the kitchen. A rare twinge of loneliness rustled beneath her ribs.

Sitting at the table, plainly enjoying the concoction they had made, Mark commented, "I envy you. You have such a good life."

Evelyn never expected anyone to envy the quiet life she was now living. "I envy you, Mark. You have so much ahead of you. You can do anything. But you're right, I suppose I do have a good life. Though sometimes it feels a tad meaningless."

"What do you mean?"

She felt self-conscious of her age. This forty-one-year-old wouldn't understand. She considered sidestepping his question, but perhaps it would do her good to say it out loud. To someone other than her reflection in the lavatory mirror.

"Sometimes I feel my days are filled with nothing more than keeping my body running. Stretching and walking and rubbing cream into my wrinkles and balm into my hands." Evelyn looked at her fingers, bumpy with arthritis, and hoped her visitor wouldn't notice how dreadful they looked. She could remember inhabiting a smoothly functioning body. Mark surely couldn't fathom inhabiting a body that had borne the brunt of seven decades.

"Preparing and eating meals," she continued. "Taking my vitamins and supplements. Next thing you know, the day's gone and I haven't achieved much of anything. My life's big triumph, my Michelin star, seems preposterous now." Evelyn sighed.

"I'm sure Daisy appreciates you taking care of her," Mark said, reaching down to scratch the little dog's rump. "Isn't that an achievement?"

It didn't seem like an achievement. Daisy gave her more than she ever gave Daisy. But Mark was kind to say it, so she agreed. Then she noticed his clean plate and offered to get him more risotto.

"You're a kind person, Evelyn. You're taking care of me, too. I'd love some more if there's enough."

"There's plenty," Evelyn replied as she stood up and spooned seconds onto Mark's plate. "I just need to set some aside for Shep."

"Shep?"

"My next-door neighbor. His wife passed a few years ago, and he doesn't see so well. I sometimes bring him meals."

"How often is sometimes?"

"Just Monday through Friday. Weekends, his kids take him out. I'll bring this to him tomorrow," Evelyn said, scraping the rest of the risotto into a container for the icebox.

Mark smiled. "Seems like you've accomplished more than a Michelin star. Look at everyone you help. Not just me. There's Shep, and your mother. And don't forget the indigenous tribe. And Daisy. I bet we aren't the only ones."

Evelyn felt her cheeks turning pink. "Well," she said, "I do volunteer at the food bank twice a month."

"A prominent chef volunteering at the food bank – that's amazing! What else?"

Mark was undoubtedly flattering her. But surely he was being considerate, not currying favor so he could take advantage of her. And she rather enjoyed this exercise. "I suppose there's also the guinea pigs," she offered.

"Guinea pigs?"

"I foster them sometimes, when they have a surplus at the animal shelter. The one where I adopted Daisy. Of course I have to keep them where she can't reach."

"And what else?"

Evelyn scooped a forkful of risotto and took a moment to chew before adding, "The spiders?"

"You foster spiders?"

Evelyn heard herself giggling. "Not exactly! It's just

that I don't kill them when I find them inside. I catch them, and then I set them free outdoors." This sounded ridiculous to Evelyn as it came out of her mouth, and her giggle turned into a chuckle.

"Really? All insects?"

"Sure," Evelyn responded, her chuckle turning into a full-fledged laugh. "Well, not mosquitoes. I'm not that crazy."

Mark laughed along with her. "I think you should feel proud of everything, Evelyn. Not just the Michelin star."

"Well, thank you, Mark. But don't make me sound like a saint. I have plenty of flaws. There's so much more I should have done in my life. There's more I should be doing now."

"It's what you do that matters, not what you don't do."

"Is that a quote from the first Mark Twain?"

"No, it's a quote from Mark Twain Chatterjee. You can look it up!" He beamed at her, and she beamed back.

After supper, Mark freshened up in the lavatory. Evelyn went to the bedroom, unlocked her nightstand drawer, removed the little box in back, ran her fingertip across Aunt Lillian's diamond. It did comfort Evelyn so to have the ring nearby. Yet, she had no real need for it. Surely Mark didn't come here to swindle her. He hadn't asked for anything. Besides, even if his intentions weren't pure, Evelyn's were. Helping someone achieve his dream could never be a foolish thing. She wrote a note on pale pink paper, gave the ring a final gaze, then placed both items into a sky-blue envelope and sealed it with her lavender "E." She tossed the key inside the nightstand drawer; no need to lock it now.

"Mark?" she called. "Do you have time to change one last lightbulb? In the bedroom?"

He came in carrying a fresh bulb, Daisy trailing behind. Evelyn pointed to the light fixture, then headed to the front hallway and slipped the envelope into Mark's knapsack.

Later that night, after watching the Lavender Express rumble by, Evelyn stood in the lavatory smoothing cream over her face. Each crease stirred an unfamiliar feeling of gratitude. The silver-haired woman looking back at her smiled. So did the fetching girl inside. Evelyn smiled back and told them both: "Maybe we can stop pondering what the measure of a life is. Maybe it's the spiders. The guinea pigs. Daisy. Shep. The food bank. Maybe it's taking care of Mother. Maybe it's leaving property to the Indian – I mean indigenous – tribe that belongs here, or maybe that won't even count once it's actually done. But it is most certainly lending a davenport – and gifting a ring – to a young man who tumbled off the Lavender Express."

With that, she retired to the bedroom, changed into her pale pink flannel pajamas, ignored the nightstand, scooted Daisy over, then paused before getting into bed.

Evelyn took out another piece of pale pink paper, another sky-blue envelope, and wrote another note: *Dear Flora, I've been thinking about you. I miss you.* She addressed the envelope and sealed it with her lavender "E." Evelyn would mail it first thing in the morning. For now, she tucked herself beneath the pink and blue patchwork quilt and closed her eyes.

About the author

Sara Winslow is a repenting (a.k.a. retired) government lawyer turned creative writer. Her work appears in several journals and anthologies. Sara lives in San Francisco. She has visited all 50 states and is working on the seven continents (two to go).

You can find her on Instagram @winslow_writing.

Nativity

Marcia Sachs

Caspar was the cat, and he was very wise, if a bit self-centred. Balthazar was the dog; he was not wise at all, but he was very faithful, or would have been, given a chance. He was, in fact, a hound, and there was nothing in his life but to sit out in the yard and bay at the moon, or even at the stars. Caspar would join him there after being put out when the house was locked up for the night. When he was in the mood, he would join his caterwauling to Balthazar's howls. Luckily there were no neighbours, or too far away to be bothered.

But Caspar was bothered by Balthazar's angst, and would have liked to get to the bottom of it. The hound was not very explicit, his howls being more or less uniform protests of anguish and grief. So Caspar studied the situation.

He noticed that dogs, as a whole, were not free. Not like himself and cats in general. As he roamed the rooftops by day or by night he saw lots of dogs, and they were always tied to something, either chained in their yard, like Balthazar, or fastened by a leash to the arm of their human. (Caspar would never have admitted to calling Melchior, the human who lived in his house and who fed him, his "master", and would not allow his friend Balathasar to suffer such indignity either. In fact, as a regular meal-provider, Melchior fell somewhat short of the mark, but Caspar had heard how hard it was to get decent help these days.) For that reason, Caspar thanked whoever it was who created him (he did recognize a nebulous superior being, otherwise where would the food come from?) for having made him a cat, and thus superior to all other creatures. And he thought it was too bad too that Melchior did not think to take Balthazar for walks, at least. He tried to argue the man into compliance, but Melchior was stupid, as most humans were, and did not understand the message. He seemed to prefer staying in the house day in and day out, most of the time in a foul temper.

One cold December night, Balthazar abruptly stopped his howling, his eye fixed on something over his head. Caspar looked too, and there high in the sky he saw a particularly brilliant star. A star with a tail – was it then a cat or a dog, in reality? It was too far away for verification. He'd heard the humans talking about making a wish – silly idea, but why not try it for once? With a piercing meow, he wished for Balthazar's chain to break. And it did.

When Balthazar began running and hopping around the yard, letting out whoops of something like joy, the door to the house was wrenched open and there stood Melchior.

"What the hell is going on here?"

He took the steps three at a time and reaching Balthazar seized the chain with both hands, soon catching on, however, that there was no way of chaining the hound up again. Balthazar had calmed down, and stood there watching the human, as if wondering what was to happen next.

"I'll have to go to the hardware store," grumbled the man. "And I'll have to take this guy with me."

He fastened the chain more securely around his wrist and went out the gate. Caspar was not to be left behind and scampered after them. Next thing they all knew was Melchior racing down the street, not on his own steam but yanked along by Balthazar who was, apparently, having the time of his life, with Caspar loping along behind them. Caspar could have been anxious: were they leaving him?

But it seemed more like a great lark, and he followed with enthusiasm.

As for Melchior, as he puffed away, trying to keep his balance, his thoughts were in a whirl. He hadn't been out, not really out, in months, not since... since when? The nippy air was sweeping those clouds of despondency from his brain, fogged up from months of being closed in with his demons, filling his waste bin with crumpled paper, and to what end? And he began to have fleeting memories of something pleasant, a girl he had met, when? Name of Marian, Marilyn, Maryam? He couldn't remember, and certainly not with this hellhound dragging him down the street as if he were on an Olympic sprint. Then the dog stopped, on a dime. Melchior almost went flying head over heels.

As soon as he recovered his balance, he saw that the dog was looking towards a house, and whining softly. When he too looked that way, he realized that a woman was tapping at the window. Tapping furiously at the window. He came closer and read on her face what seemed to be a call for help. She was gesturing towards the door, so he went that way and as he reached it, a buzzer sounded. He pushed the door and it opened.

In the hallway another door opened and the woman stood just inside it, or rather, crouched, seemingly in great pain. As he approached she stood up again with a deep sigh and seemed to pull herself together. She was awfully fat, he noticed as she motioned him to advance.

"Come in, come in," she said with considerable urgency. "I need you."

Need me? She doesn't know me from Adam. But she didn't give him much time to wonder. She thrust a basin into his hands.

"Fill this with hot water. But wash your hands first.

104

With soap. And the pets (Pets? he thought), in there." She gestured towards what must be a sitting room before disappearing herself into another.

Caspar was delighted by the sitting room, and jumped onto a red plush sofa from which he had a view into the next room. Balthazar, suddenly tired out from his unwonted exercise, laid his head on his paws and began to snooze.

When Melchior came back with the basin he saw that there was already a pile of soft white towels. He set it next to them, and looked round for the woman. She was just about to sit down on a rickety old chair or so it seemed.

"Stop!" he cried out. "There's no seat!"

But she was shaking her head, her face contorted once again with pain. "It's all right," she gasped, and sure enough when she sat down she did not go through. What the devil was going on?

She motioned him to kneel down in front of her, which he did with some trepidation, and then she said, "Take hold of him when he starts coming, but gently, no squeezing. Get him under the ears, and help him out."

What the heck? And then she was groaning again, almost a howl. Was she dying? Or turning into a hound? Was this some magical nightmare he had fallen into? But after a moment she relaxed again.

"Don't worry," she said. "I'm a trained midwife. I'll tell you what to do."

What to do? What to do in what? And what the devil was a midwife? But then she was screaming again.

"He's coming! He's coming! Get him!"

Where? Where? Melchior looked around himself in a panic. But she was pointing down between her legs. And then he saw it. A tiny head, with a face. Something clicked: a baby. He jumped forward, and gently gently, surprising even himself, he eased the baby out, too late realizing how wet and slippery it was. He threw a look to the woman for some of the promised advice, but she was collapsing in relief, her eyes shut. Then they opened, full of clarity and direction.

"You have to wash him, and wrap him up in that cloth."

As he began to turn away, she said sharply, "But you have to cut the cord first!"

That was when he saw that the infant was attached to its mother by a cord. Not quite panicking he looked around and saw a pair of scissors. Picking them up, and without hesitation, he cut the cord. After which he plunged the baby, which had begun to scream, into the warm water and washed it all over, which stopped its howling, then took it out and bundled it into one of the towels. Only then did he realize he had just cut into human flesh and had also performed some other actions he had never done before.

The woman had got up from the chair and was making her way to the bed, onto which she collapsed and then held out her arms for the packet, which he readily gave her.

"Christ," he said. "That was awful."

"No, it wasn't," she said back. "It was wonderful." She looked down fondly into the packet for a moment. Then she thrust it toward him. "And this is yours."

He pulled back, what was this? He'd done his bit, even though touching that slimy creature was something he would never have done had it not been in the urgency of the moment. And even if, now washed and wrapped up nicely, it was not so repellent, what was she doing foisting it off on him?

"You'll have to give it back of course," she said, "because it's also mine. But just take a good look at it. At him, I mean, because as you saw for yourself, it's a boy."

Not quite understanding, but with her compelling eyes

upon him, he took the packet, which was warm and light, and very still, its perfectly formed eyes shut. Then they opened, grey eyes flicked with yellow, fringed with long black lashes, and they looked straight at him. A look like an arrow shot.

"They're your eyes," she said.

What nonsense was she talking? "My eyes are black," he said, and looked down at the baby's, which had shut again.

"Dark brown. And these eyes will darken with time, just wait and see."

What was she going on about, wait and see? He didn't intend to wait around any longer than necessary. He'd done his bit. And now it was time he was going, say his farewell and all that.

"Er, ah, what did you say your name was?"

"I didn't, but you should know it."

He recoiled again, but she continued. "Myriam."

And when he didn't react, she went on, "The Easter picnic? You were pretty drunk but oh so gentle."

Him? Gentle? What Easter picnic? Then a vague memory of sunshine and green grass and a spread at the local parish social, that he went to because a mate (who, again? he hadn't seen any mates in a long time) had said there would be lots of food, lots of beer, and, yes, that pretty girl who, now that he looks at her more carefully, resembled this woman not by half. He suddenly feels trapped by this memory he doesn't fully comprehend.

"You... you're Myriam?" Yes, that was it.

"And that's Joshua." At its name, the packet broke into wails, and he was about to thrust it back where it came from, but then the wails stopped, as suddenly as Balthazar's howls had earlier, the infant opened its eyes again and gazed into his, and then smiled. Smiled! He felt something melt in his gut. He stood there, rooted to the spot. Their eyes locked for fully half a minute. Then he hurriedly relinquished the packet into the arms of its mother. This was too confusing.

"I'd often seen you before, all closed up and surly. Then at the picnic, you were so different. I thought you would phone me afterwards, but I guess you were too drunk to take the paper with my number. You never did call. And I never saw you again, till tonight. Are you a recluse?"

"Not professionally," he said, and surprised himself at the formulation. "I'm a writer."

"I know. Melchior? Isn't that it? I never found any work by you on the internet."

"That's because I've never published," he replied gruffly.

"Oh, dear me," she said. "That must be seen to."

What the devil was she doing meddling with his life?

"Don't frown," she said. "I just meant, you need someone to encourage you, and take care of the practical stuff."

It was like a dart that hit the target right in the middle of his chest. That was exactly what he had been saying to himself earlier in the day. He just wasn't meant for the business side of writing. He softened, rather suddenly, feeling like something that had been tossed around violently in a clothes-dryer and now came out all spineless and spongy like a teddy bear.

"Sit down," she said. "You've had a hard time."

He'd had a hard time? What about her? She looked tired, yes, but radiant. He had to hand it to her, she had pluck. And she looked so happy. It was catching.

"Tell me more about the picnic," he said.

And, tucking the baby under her breast for its first feeding, with Casper the cat perked up and listening greedily and Balthazar still snoozing, she began.

About the author

Marcia Sachs (a pseudonym) was born and educated in the United States, but has lived most of her adult life elsewhere, in Mexico and especially in Europe. She has been writing since childhood, but has only recently decided to try publishing some of her work. She has worked twenty years as a teacher and has three grown children.

Quizmas Rivalry

Paula R. C. Readman

The snow was falling faster now, blanketing the ground, and coating the hedge that bordered the King's Head car park and the main road out of the village. The King's Head, an old coaching inn, with accommodation for weary travellers, always greeted them with a real fire in the hearth on cold winter nights. Every Thursday, the King's Head hosted a pub quiz, competing against other pub teams until the end of the year, when the two surviving teams faced a head-to-head challenge.

Typical, Mel thought as he gazed out the pub window. Of all nights, it had to snow tonight. He had waited an entire year to reclaim the challenge cup from their rivals, Gabriel's Shepherds, and now it looked like they might have to cancel the Christmas pub quiz. The Shepherds, three-man team from The Angel pub in the next village had taken the trophy from The Three Wise Men of the King's Head for the last three years, leaving Mel and his friends feeling like underdogs in the competition. Mel couldn't understand why the rest of his team took it so lightly as he continued to stare at the falling snow – this time, they had to defeat the Shepherds.

"I'm sure, it's our time to out shine them – if only it would stop snowing," Mel muttered.

"Come away from the window, Mel. Wishful thinking won't change the weather," said Pete, the pub's proprietor.

"Why did it have to snow today? Tomorrow wouldn't matter," Mel replied, turning to face him.

"That's life," Pete said, giving the bar another quick wipe.

"You'll wear that cloth out, Pete; it's the third time you've wiped the bar down!"

"Habit. Anyway, we can always postpone the competition until after Christmas," he suggested.

"What, and give the Shepherds another reason to mock us?" Mel retorted.

"You're taking this far too personally, Mel."

Mel shook his head. "They've won the cup three times in a row now. I just want to wipe the smug looks off their faces."

Pete tossed his cleaning cloth in Mel's direction and, with a grin said, "Relax. Remember, tomorrow the new King is born."

Mel caught the damp cloth and smiled. "Yes, that's all well and good, but when you have a brother like Herod continually joking about how the so-called wise men aren't so wise, it becomes repetitive."

Before Pete could respond with some witty remark, the outer door swung open, bringing in a blast of cold air, and excited voices. The Shepherds had arrived, along with their entourage. They were always dressed for any occasion, as their leader often declared – they were "dressed to kill."

"Hello, dear brother! The reigning winners have arrived!" Herod announced to the half-filled pub, placing the small silver cup on the bar. "Not many in tonight."

"The weather won't help. Are you and your team having your usual drinks?" Pete asked.

"Of course, my good man, but still, we'll have an enjoyable evening winning the cup.

"By the end of the night, it will be ours again, brother," Mel said, offering a smile.

Herod patted his brother on the back. "It will be a fair fight, brother. I must join my team now."

Mel narrowed his eyes as he watched Herod join the others. Since Herod had left home and moved to the neighbouring village, he had formed new friendships, while

Mel had remained loyal to his old friends and childhood home – a place familiar to him.

There had always been rivalry between the two brothers since they were children. Mel was sure Herod saw it as light-hearted fun, but he had grown tired of being the butt of his jokes. For three years at the family Christmas get-together, Mel endured Herod's little jibes about how the three wise men from the King's Head wouldn't be able to follow the star even if they had satnav.

"Mel, sorry I'm late." Frank said, snapping Mel out of his thought. Mel, Frank, and Adrian were long-time friends, who had been through many scrapes together over the years. Mel smiled at his friends' wives as they greeted his girlfriend, Irene.

"I see Herod is already throwing his orders around," Frank remarked, gesturing to Pete that he was ready to order.

"Lais! Help me move those tables ready for the quiz master's arrival." Herod's voice boomed across the room to where his team were sitting.

"Where's Henry?" Mel asked Frank as he helped him carry the drinks over to where the women were.

"He's on his way. Just running a bit late – you know how it is. You never leave your place of work on time, especially at this time of the year icy roads and pavements."

"I hope he makes it on time. We can't have the team down a member."

"Don't panic. He'll be here."

"We have to win back the cup tonight; otherwise, Herod will be intolerable at dinner tomorrow."

"Ah, a good old-fashioned Christmas dinner – the old traditions are the best. You should relax more, Mel, and take it in your stride. You know, he does it to wind you up. Your poor parents are going to a lot of trouble to give you a great time, and there you two are bickering like kids."

"You're right, but it's still annoying. Mum always sits me opposite him. It's unbearable seeing his smug face and listening to his snide remarks all through dinner."

"Be the grown up for your parents, Mel. Oh, look, here comes Henry. Henry, over here." Frank signalled to Henry and his girlfriend, "Hi Jenny."

Once the seats were all in place, Pete hung two small signs at the front of each table so the audience knew which team was which. As the teams took to their seats, Pete placed the buzzers on the table next to the players.

"What are the roads like?" Pete asked Henry as he checked to ensure each buzzer was working.

"Not too bad now that the winds dropped. Hopefully, a few more people will arrive to watch us win the cup back," Henry replied, humour edging his voice.

"Wishful thinking, Henry," Herod said with a laugh.

"I think it is ours this time," Henry replied confidently.

Pete walked over to the bar and rang the bell. "Could I have everyone's attention? Thank you all for battling your way through this awful weather. As soon as the quizmaster arrives, we will be ready to start. Please could the two teams take their seats now? If you need drinks, or refreshment, fetch them now or go through to the public bar.

Soon the pub was buzzing as everyone took their seats after fetching drinks. The quizmaster arrived and set up his iPad on the table between the two teams. The adjudicator took a seat next to the quizmaster to keep the score.

"Is everyone ready?" Pete asked. The teams nodded. "Let the fun begin." Pete rang the last-order bell.

"The first question," said the quizmaster. "Who composed the music for *The Messiah*?

Mel hit the buzzer first. "George Frideric Handel."

"Yes," said the quizmaster.

"Second question: who wrote the Picture of Dorian Gray?"

Lais hit his buzzer. "Oscar Wilde."

"Yes. Next question: Who wrote the classic story *A Christmas Carol*?

Herod and Mel both hit their buzzer at the same time, but the adjudicator called Mel's name first.

"Charles Dickens."

"Yes, fourth question: How many tips does a snowflake usually have?

Frank on the Wise Men team hit his buzzer. "Six."

"Brilliant." Mel slapped his friend on the back.

Questions came quickly, followed by the sound of the buzzer. First, one team answered, then the other – back and forth. The Shepherds took the lead, but the Wise Men quickly reclaimed it. A hush fell over the crowd, heightening the tension in the room. Mel felt confident the cup would finally be theirs.

"Now for the tiebreaking question. The first team to provide the correct answer wins. Are you ready?" the quizmaster asked. Herod grinned at his brother while Mel refused to meet his gaze. "In which year was the first Christmas card sent?"

Muttering spread through both teams. Just as the team captains raised their hands above their buzzers, the pub door burst open, and a man rushed in, his face flushed. "The baby is on its way! My car has broken down in a snowdrift. I need a doctor!"

"I am," Mel jumped to his feet, forgetting the cup. "Show me where?" He followed the man outside as Herod pulled out his phone and called an ambulance.

"Accident blocking the road, okay, I understand. My brother is a newly qualified doctor, and is with her now. She's in the car. Right, I'll tell him." Herod turned to Pete. "We need to bring the mother-to-be inside to keep her warm. Is there anywhere suitable to deliver the baby if necessary? It might take a while for an ambulance to get through as a serious accident has blocked the main road."

"Oh, we could use one of the bedrooms upstairs," Pete suggested.

"There won't be time for that," Mel replied as he brought the father-to-be and his wife in from the cold.

"What if we brought one of the mattresses down here? At least it'll be more comfortable," Irene suggested. Suddenly, everyone sprang into action, fetching the mattress downstairs and rearranging the furniture in one of the snugs to create a makeshift delivery room. Pete's wife, Carol, brought down some sheets and towels while Jenny carried a jug of hot water and a large bowl from the kitchen. The sheets soon became curtains to provide some privacy for the mother-to-be. Mel and Irene, a trainee nurse, disappeared behind the curtains while the regulars at the King's Head waited.

When Pete announced, "Time, ladies and gentlemen, please," many of the patrons who had arrived on foot left, but few remained. Pete turned off the beer taps, covering them with bar towels before gathering the dirty glasses. Carol and some of the other wives brought out trays of sandwiches for those who were staying.

"It's going to be a long night," Pete said, carrying a tray filled with snacks and sandwiches. He joined Henry and his wife, Jenny, as they finished their meals.

"Pete, am I correct that you told us that this part of the inn was once the old stable block before it was converted?" Jenny asked as she nibbled on her sandwich.

"Yes, that's correct. It dates back to the 13th century."

"That's interesting. So what's happening now is reminiscent of the first Christmas –you know when a child was born in a stable in Bethlehem."

"What are you saying, Jen," Henry asked, trying to ignore the moans and groans coming from behind the curtain as Mel encouraged the mother-to-be to push.

"Well, we have the three Wise Men, the Shepherds, and the star over the stable, plus a child in a manger. Okay, so that isn't quite true, but there is a star." Jenny pointed to Christmas decorations over the makeshift delivery room.

Everyone looked to where Jenny was pointing. A five-pointed foil star shone in the firelight.

"Oh, my goodness, the star I put up." Pete laughed.

Just then, a cry rang out as the clock struck midnight.

"The child is born on Christmas day," everyone cheered.

Mel drew the curtain back. The sight that greeted the remaining regulars of the King's Head was the new parents, the father's arm around his wife's shoulder as she cradled their newborn child. Mel beamed and announced, "Dov and Zara would like you all to welcome their son into the world."

"We should wet the baby's head!" Pete raised his glass as Carol and Jenny carried trays of drinks to everyone.

Jenny raised her glass and asked the proud father, "Dov, does your son have a name yet?"

Dov looked down at his wife, who smiled at him. "We are naming him after my father – Joseph, Joseph King."

Mel laughed and said, "You were right, Pete. A new king was born today!"

Once the Kings and their baby, Joseph, were safely in the ambulance on their way to the hospital, Mel and Irene joined Jenny, Henry, and Herod for food and drink.

Herod put his arm around his brother's shoulder. "You were amazing. Seeing you in action made me so proud, little brother."

"Thank you, but I had a great team at my side." Mel hugged Irene.

"I hope you're bringing Irene to Mum and Dad's later because I want to share with them the amazing thing you two did today. You were so calm while delivering your first baby."

"Just doing our job, brother," Mel said, "though, it's not every day that one gets to deliver a new King into the world on Christmas day."

"Better than winning the cup off us," Herod said, raising his glass.

"Always next year, dear brother," Mel laughed. "Happy Christmas, everyone!"

About the author

Paula R. C. Readman is a prolific writer and has penned six books and over a hundred short stories. She lives in an Essex village with her husband, Russell.

Blog: https://colourswordspaper.blog or just Google Paula R C Readman, and something's bound to pop up.

Return of the Magi

Richard A. Ballou

The Magi came again this year, bearing strange gifts. A large empty box. A house with no rooms. And a side order of grits.

They didn't announce themselves. I just heard the commotion at the side entrance and the clamour of camels as they made their way up the garage stairs and into the kitchen. The house was bare except for my bed, and so the hullabaloo echoed throughout every corner. It was a wickedly bright morning, especially in the dining room, which faces the east and yet was presently stripped of even its curtains and blinds. I hated that room now which had once been my favourite. The Magi and their humpbacks chose to assemble there this year.

Since they awoke me from a dead sleep, I had yet to shower or shave and had thrown on yesterday's clothes. I looked distraught, in no shape to accept guests. If they had sent word ahead of time like usual, I could have gotten things in order a bit. I could have dispatched a note informing the roving royals of the disjointed state of my affairs. At least they would have known. Maybe that's why they came unannounced – because they *did* know.

My home is, of course, grand and spacious. Years ago when I first saw it, the house was still under construction. I bought it in time for the builder to expand and revise the layout to make it custom to my needs and my growing family's needs. I've always needed space, lots of space, and variety, plenty of it. So, I spared no expense. A wide array of the finest fixtures and luxury appointments, marble and hardwood floors with intricate inlaid designs, crown mouldings with exquisite detailing, oversized rooms (all sorts of them), and ten-foot ceilings throughout. In its present empty state, I guess it is a pretty good place for Magi to assemble. With the high ceilings and broad hallways, it's easy to get camels in and out now that the furniture's gone.

Empty or not, the Magi wouldn't be staying the evening. They never do. They usually come and mill about the five-car garage and talk about how good it is to convene once again at the final destination. I let them hang out there in the morning talking their strange talk and resting their animals. Then I come down shortly before noon, and we do the gift thing.

Walking into the huge, two-story foyer on the way to the dining room, I thought, *Damn. I have no gifts for them this year.* They don't necessarily come on Christmas day, you see. One year they did. But mostly it's as much as a week before or even a week later. That's why it's important for them to send me some advance notice so I know what day they'll be here at the earliest. So, I can have something for them. Not to mention the hay for the camels. I usually clean up the garage and move out any valuable stuff that might get knocked around by the ungainly beasts. I didn't have to do that this year.

I reached for my cell phone, but remembered it had disappeared with all the rest of the stuff. So, I took a quick detour around to the kitchen. Luckily, there was still a phone in there, and it was still connected. I called around to a few places in the area to see if anyone could deliver some hay. After haggling with a guy I have done business with for years, he said he could get some over but not for a few hours. For an extra seventy-five bucks, no less. Had to hire out the job, he claimed, since his delivery guy was already booked for the day. That would have to do. Certainly, I thought, the three kings would understand, given their arrival was so sudden.

119

What day is this, I wondered? And why did they not send their normal card? All embossed and in an exotic, gilded font, it usually read:

We three kings of Orient are
Beating a path to your home from afar.
We should be there on this date, *(date here)*,
And depart no later than eight.
We have gifts and tidings too.
Forward we look to seeing you soon.

Reverentially,
Buck, Showboat, and Ramirez
(my nicknames for them)

Well, this makes no sense at all, I thought to myself as I headed back towards the dining room. The Magi are very formal in nature and also quite orderly, so why not the standard announcement? Maybe it had gotten lost in the move. Or she had taken it by mistake when she came by for the mail.

She, of course, is my estranged wife who took everything (and I mean everything) about a week earlier. I hadn't been very lucid since. I hadn't been drunk either. Mostly in a state of shock and delirium. It made no sense that she should leave like that. I hadn't screamed at her (or the kids for that matter) in over a month. And my drinking was under control. And in the week leading up to her surprise departure, I hadn't even had a woman in the house. Didn't even go looking for one. It was downright depressing how reformed I had become.

And then she leaves. Talk about depressed. Since she took all the stuff that fateful evening she knew I was going to be out late, I had not had a woman either. In fact, that night I wasn't even out past 3:00 AM. (It must have been something of a SWAT-like job – two or three giant moving vans and twenty to thirty high-performance movers dressed in black ninja outfits with infrared helmet lights to see in the dark and everything out of here in no more than three hours flat.) No, since that catastrophic event I had not so much as glanced at the opposite sex. Now that's depressed. I couldn't remember being so forlorn since I had that nasty little problem with my testicles.

Anyway, I didn't want the Magi to be upset at me for not being prepared – especially if they had sent an advance notice. Although I can be pretty thoughtless of others, I always gave the Magi their due. I always did the right thing by them. As I walked around to the dining room, I wondered what they were thinking, about the emptiness and there being no hay in the garage. It was, of course, not normal for them to parade their means of transportation into the house like that. But they're from foreign lands; and when they saw the garage empty, they must have figured for some reason that the hay was in the house. I guess they settled in the dining room because it was the closest room with the most space. It has a vaulted ceiling, and you can easily fit a table long enough for a dozen Magi to dine in style, with elbow room to spare. And, unlike the rest of the house, it was almost warm in there with the large windows, the absence of curtains and blinds, and the direct morning sunlight. (I was keeping the thermostat real low to conserve energy. It seemed the thing to do, given the reduced lifestyle I potentially faced.)

The Magi are pretty classy guys and all, they're being kings of a sort. But they are foreign, as I said, and still don't have the hang of America. That was the only explanation I could think of for why they had let a couple of the camels relieve themselves right on the vintage hardwood floor. When I came into the room, I had to sidestep a big pile of excrement; and I heard a hard pissing noise off in one of the corners where the camels were now herded.

I was trying to think of something that might be around that I could give them as gifts, but that pissing sound really had unnerved me. I was about to say something in a peeved tone when Buck announced, "We can't stay long, you know. It's really quite cold in here."

"I'm sorry," I said. "There's been a problem. But I can't explain. I really haven't figured it out yet myself, you know."

"Of course," said Showboat. "These things happen. Still, we would like to present your gifts and see the child if we may. We can dispense with the traditional pleasantries if you understand."

"Sure, sure," I said. But I was now thinking, *What about the child? I'm not sure I can produce the child.* Well, it didn't matter right away. They always offered the gifts to me first. To get my approval. Then we would talk a little about the state of the world – the price of commodities, the confluence of cultures, how difficult it was to get decent myrrh these days – and I would casually bestow some presents on them. My stuff was never anything expensive or elaborate like theirs was, and it wasn't picked out expressly for them like their gifts to me; so I wasn't *that* worried. Except I didn't have anything in the house.

Well, my wife *had* left the refrigerator behind. And there were still some leftovers in there. Food could be a gift, couldn't it? Perhaps some petits fours from the last party were tucked away in a back corner. Then it hit me – no, no, no, that wasn't necessary. There was the secret vault in the attic recess. It was one of those special design features I had added. No one but the builder and the carpenter and I knew. Among other things I had some stuff stashed away in there for last-second Christmas presents. You know, for those brief, spur-of-the-moment holiday flings.

Collectibles! I would give them each a three-inch, hand-painted, pewter Santa collectible! Numbered and authenticated limited editions, of course.

The hard pissing sound had now stopped. Which is probably why I could think on my feet again. But now the odour was beginning to get to me. I looked at the three Magi, and they were growing ever-more serious in their expressions. Especially Ramirez. He was downright frowning. And he was nodding. That was like Ramirez. He nodded a lot. He never said anything. Maybe because he couldn't speak English. At least I didn't think he could. Certainly, he was the most ethnic looking of the three. But it occurred to me then that with all the nodding maybe he was really mute.

Anyway, next thing I knew they were all frowning, as if they had figured something out. It was then that Ramirez handed me the side order of grits.

"What's this?" I asked.

"I believe you call them grits, Mr. O. I believe you call them grits," Buck said for him.

Ramirez was holding his hands out, and his frown had now grown into a threatening stare. This was not the usual protocol for gift-giving for sure. And what was with the grits? This was not the usual gift – even from Ramirez.

"I don't understand," I said.

"They're to eat. You look like you could use some warm sustenance. He has kept them hot. They are special in that they never get cold. Eat them to show your acceptance." Again, it was Buck doing the speaking.

Well, showing acceptance was part of the protocol. But I did not want to eat those grits. Even though they were obviously fresh, a tidy cloud of steam constantly hovering above them. So, I apologized, saying I was having some indigestion. And I looked in the direction of the camels and then touched and wrinkled my nose so the Magi would get my drift. This time Showboat nodded, and so I figured it was okay to take the grits and put them away. I considered the refrigerator. But since they always stayed hot, that didn't make much sense. So, I put them on the staircase a reasonable distance from the camels.

By this time Showboat was presenting me his gift, a large box with the lid pulled back. He held it up high before me with a very formal and solemn extension of his arms. It was a pretty average box. Like the kind they put a take-out cake in or a large item from a gift shop. You know, they come flat with pre-cut slits and flaps and then you fold the sides and insert the flaps to make a box. This one was white on the outside and grey on the inside. Nothing special, just kind of big. The top was open, but after the grits I wasn't sure I wanted to look inside. But Showboat just kept holding it there and blinking his eyes as if to gesture something. He blinked a few more times to where it was almost comical. Finally, I stood on my tiptoes and peered into the box. That's what he wanted me to do.

It was empty. I never expected it to be empty. But it was. Certifiably empty. Zilch. Nada.

I looked in the box so as not to offend Showboat. (I gave him that name because he dressed the flashiest of the three – lots of colourful robes and rich, flowing scarves and stuff. He liked purples and yellows especially. And his crown was a bit overdone, too many prongs and jewels for my tastes.) Anyway, I gazed into the box not to offend him. I must have looked pretty puzzled, perhaps even dazed, because soon Buck was telling me to back away. "Too much staring at it and you could lose your wits, you know. Too much staring at it and you could even fall in." He put his arm around my shoulders and led me outside. I felt pretty low at this point. And certainly confused. I needed someone to put an arm around me. For a Magus, Buck could be a pretty personable guy.

124

We stood out front on the brick entranceway landing. At the edge of the sweeping circular drive. The sun was remarkably bright, and it was warm under its rays even though the day was very cold. I gazed at the fine, upscale brick of the house, the way it seemed to absorb and store the sun's energy, and it made me feel better. The moment I first saw it, I fell in love with that brick and the façade of the home. The strong and commanding traditional appearance. So settled in the lot. As if nothing could knock it over. And with a style that invariably looked its best during the holidays and in the clear, crisp days of winter. That's why I selected the home. Maybe that's why the Magi selected me.

We remained there for a while. I don't know how long. And Buck didn't say anything. He just stood there all imposing and majestic-like and gazed down at me. He was tall, exceptionally tall. All the kings were, but especially Buck. His arm still planted across my shoulders, I fidgeted a time or two, but Buck's grip only grew firmer. I felt safe and secure and a bit awkward and intimidated all at once.

In time, I realized he had removed his arm. Still, we lingered on, side by side, in the quiet brilliance of the day. I wanted to stand there all day like that – stationed on and before the unyielding brick, absorbing the radiant warmth of the sun, enjoying my house from the outside. The air was strikingly clean and fresh. I needed the fresh air. But now Buck was motioning me back inside. We walked up the porch stairs together, and he even held his arm out for me. I remember thinking, he must figure I'm pretty bad off. I remember thinking I had lost track of time. That maybe there was something in that empty box more than emptiness. I was going to reach out and get the door for Buck since, after all, this was my house and he was a guest.

But he beat me to it and graciously opened the door as if he were a real estate agent ushering me into a grand new property.

And when I walked in, it *was* a new place. It was still my massive abode, but now there were no interior walls. Not even any stairs or a second floor. All the rooms were gone. All the windows were still in place and the carpet and marble and hardwood floors in perfect condition. The paint on the perimeter walls was without blemish, as if nothing had happened. But all my rooms were gone.

I was stunned, to say the least. But not so stunned to have forgotten my gifts to them. Oh my god, I thought. I can't get to the secret attic vault. There's no way up there now, if it even still exists. The refrigerator was still in the kitchen, though, which was largely intact except for the walls. The petits fours would have to do. I didn't suspect the Magi would be offended, given the circumstances. They never came for the gifts anyway. They wanted to see the child.

But there was no child in the house now. Their gifts had ensured that. There had hardly been a child around for a while anyway, though. The changes I had made in myself shortly before my wife and kids left pretty much ran him off.

I remember Buck saying as they rode the camels up the driveway and prepared to make the first right turn on their long journey back: "You should get some sleep. Enjoy the gifts tomorrow. By the way, we won't be returning next year of course. But if the child should one day come back, we will know, and we will return. We trust it will not."

Ramirez nodded and Showboat looked quite king-like. As they marched down the street, the truck with the hay passed them in front of the house. The driver gave them no notice, not the slightest turn of the head, just proceeded beyond the driveway a bit and then took a wide turn to back in. I told him I didn't need the hay after all. He told me I still had to pay the delivery charge.

About the author
Richard A. Ballou is a former executive with a multinational IT-consulting firm. He retired from the technology world in his mid-forties to write literary fiction. His stories have been finalists or top-three finishers in numerous international contests, including the Calvino Prize, the Omnidawn Fabulist Fiction Chapbook Contest, the Doris Betts Fiction Competition, the Press 53 Open Awards, the Opossum Prize, and the annual contest sponsored by the *Vincent Brothers Review*. Richard's work has appeared in a variety of literary anthologies and periodicals. His writing goal is to engage and entertain while challenging and stretching the reader's field of vision.

Seosamh, Meryem, the Busker and the Boy

Steve Wade

Pitching their tent in the scrubland next to the low cliffs above the sea had its good and bad points. For Seosamh (pronounced show-siv), the good outweighed the bad. They were away from the nearby town, with its noise and threats from people on the street. For the extra cash he got when tapping and working with his pots and pans, the constant tirade of abuse that came at him, night and day, wasn't worth it. Apart from the usual name calling, late-night revellers would roar and shout as they lay trembling in their dirty sleeping bags. The revellers threw bottles and cans at their tent, tried to set it alight. And worse.

The blustery, sometimes near gale-force, winds that often raged inward from the Atlantic, battering and slashing at the thin walls of their tent, were preferable over the human threat on the streets.

Christmas Eve morning. Seosamh insisted that Meryem stay where she was. Keep warm in her sleeping bag and under the duvet. He'd get her a spot of breakfast before he left. She didn't need to be getting sick, especially with the baby due to arrive any day now. She smiled, but he could see the terrible sadness in her eyes. He kissed her cheek, the soft flesh giving on his chapped lips.

Outside the tent the cold pounced on him like a predator. He pulled the hood of his hoodie over his head and tightened the drawstring. A light dusting of snow had drifted on one side of the two-person Sundome tent and frozen solid. And frozen too to the earth was the plastic container on which sat a concrete block. Around the container were tiny pawprints, rat tracks, and the swish prints of tails in the snow. And he could smell the pungent smell of rodent urine. It tickled the inside of his nostrils.

He shifted the concrete block from atop the container. But when he tried to remove the lid, it was stuck fast. To defrost it, he did what he had to do. He needed to empty his bladder anyway.

The lid peeled away with a clunk. He brought it to his nose and smelled the contents, the opened packets of rashers and sausages. Just a slightly sour odour. A few days out of date, this was normal. Once they were cooked, they'd be fine. Next he upended a large mayonnaise container, the yellowed grass beneath dryish. From a few plastic bags he took some sticks, tinder, and kindling. The tinder bundle he placed in the centre of the pit enclosed by four rocks. Onto this he put some kindling. Next he put a stick in the middle of the bundle and built a tepee of sticks around it.

From behind the dry-stone wall near where they had pitched their tent, Dekel the donkey's head appeared.

"Hey Dekel," Seosamh said. "Good morning, sir. It's a cold one, isn't it?" He cupped his hands and blew into them. Meryem had given the donkey the name.

The donkey brayed, which set off the bleating of the black lamb where it watched, sticking close to its surrogate mother, the fawn-coloured cow, from outside the cowshed in the corner of the field.

The first match Seosamh struck fizzled out as soon as it fired. He swallowed. There were just a few matches left in the box. He took two and struck them together and waited for the tiny flame to grip. Careful not to inadvertently exhale, he brought it to the kindling. The kindling smoked and flamed for a bit before dying as the matches were spent. He blew on the few wisps that were smouldering yet.

"No, please, light, light."

It didn't.

"Don't worry about me, love," Meryam called out from inside the tent. "I'll be fine till you get back."

"It's okay, cuisle mo chroí – *pulse of my heart*. You need hot food inside you."

He drew another match across the box's striking surface. The tiny flame bloomed, and this time it locked onto the kindling and took right off. It burned brightly, as did the stick tepee. With the fire safely established, he took from the container one of the last few logs he had seasoned naturally during the warmer summer months. The logs he had hidden in a strong plastic bag in a bramble bush.

Once the fire burned steadily, he placed the blackened grate over it, its edges supported by the rocks. The equally blackened teapot he filled with water from the litre and a half Coke bottle. Around the teapot he laid the two sausages and three rashers. To keep them from burning he turned them continuously.

The appetising aroma lifting off the cooking food mingled with the air. Seosamh swallowed, his throat contracting. When cooked, he used a piece of a branch to fork the rashers and sausages onto a children's green plastic plate. A warm sensation bubbled inside him as he crouched and pulled aside the tent flap.

"Are you awake, mo stor?" – *my treasure*?

Meryem turned her head on the pillow, her sleepy eyes crowded with confused love, Seosamh thought. He could imagine how she viewed him right then. A man she had given up her family to be with when tectonic plates shifted beneath the earth in her homeland. When they met, Seosamh had been backpacking around Europe. Doing odd jobs. They had fled the crumbling buildings together, the devastation, the horror, the putrid stench of death, the eking out an existence in government-provided tents to cross the sea to his birthplace and ended up living together in an even flimsier tent.

No safe room behind locked doors. No warm dry bed with clean sheets.

He placed the plate of food on the floor of the tent and helped Meryem to sit up. Their two pillows he plumped up behind her back.

"Now," he said, putting the green plate in her lap, and a plastic knife and fork in her hands. "Get that into you, mo storín." *my little darling*. The sausages and rashers he had already cut up. "Wait. I'll get your tea."

"But where's your breakfast, tatlim?" – *sweetheart*? she said when he crawled back into the tent with her tea in a chipped white mug depicting a beaming, red-cheeked Santa.

"I'm good," he said. "Sure, I'll get something in McDonald's when I go into town."

She tried to insist that he take at least one of the sausages, but Seosamh smiled and shook his head. He'd be fine. She was the one they had to keep fed and warm.

When Meryem had finished eating, Seosamh cleaned the utensils and put them away. He then helped her to the second smaller tent they jokingly called the washroom. And he waited until she was done. Now he was ready.

He kissed her goodbye, came out of the tent and pushed to his feet. There he heaved a frayed green rucksack onto his shoulders. The pots and pan inside the bag clanged together.

"Stay warm," he said. "Don't leave the tent unless you have to. I'll bring back some fish and chips once I get enough readies, okay?"

"Be careful," she said. "Don't let anybody push you into doing something silly."

Seosamh promised his wife he'd do as she advised. She blew him a kiss. He waited until she pulled to the zip on the tent from the inside.

As he made his way down the path to the seafront, he kept

his gaze ahead of him. He could feel the disapproving eyes of those he past flicking at him like a serpent's tongue. He stopped at the first rubbish bin he came to and used the *Allen key* he carried to open it. The key he kept for this specific purpose. Two empty beer cans, and three plastic bottles. One can still had some stale beer inside. He brought his fingers to his nose where the beer had spilt and smelled them. The can he emptied over the wall onto the sand. He shook the can. The bottles and cans he put inside his rucksack.

While he made his way to his tapping patch, he collected another seventeen deposit back containers. With not enough room in his rucksack to store them, he used one of the black plastic bin liners he had to carry them. A city council worker he was on friendly terms with gave him a few bags now and then.

It came upon him without warning, as it sometimes did: light-headedness. Waves passed before his unfocused eyes. It felt as though he were coming in and out of a dream state. And he thought he might collapse. He sat down on the pavement, leaning into his rucksack the way he would the back of a sofa. His bag of plastic bottles and cans he placed beside him, a hand gripping the lip of the bag. He let his eyes close and allowed the white noise of the crowds walking through the street wash over him. Through him.

In the distance he could hear a Christmas song being piped from a shop. And passing him a mixture of languages. Besides English and Portuguese, he detected what might have been Russian, maybe Ukrainian. But it could have been Polish, or Latvian. He wouldn't recognise the subtleties.

"There you go, buddy," a male voice said.

Seosamh felt himself jumping, which embarrassed him. He had drifted off. He laughed a nervous laugh. "Sorry," he said, his eyes open as he twisted his head about to see who had spoken to him. But his vision was still unfocused. He could make out the blurry silhouette of a man in black, a guitar case swinging from his shoulder. The man turned and waved an arm. Seosamh returned the wave. That's when he noticed a takeaway cup of coffee and a paper bag on the ground beside him.

"Thanks," Seosamh shouted out to the street. "Thanks very much."

The first mouthful of coffee from the Styrofoam cup slipped down his throat like liquid sunshine. He opened the paper bag. Inside a Danish pastry. He bit into it, its succulent texture and sweet raisins in his mouth tasting right then and there like the most wonderful thing he had ever eaten. He closed his eyes while he chewed, taking sips of the coffee, the uplifting liquid melding with the pastry to reach a crescendo of piquant delight.

Not until he thought of it did he realise that his light-headedness had gone. But gone too he saw was his black sack with the deposit-returns. He cursed aloud but quickly settled himself.

Time to earn a crust. From his rucksack he took out three small saucepans of varying size and a frying pan. These he placed before him upside down on the ground. And then, with a pair of wooden spoons, he started into a rhythmic beat until he established a groove. A small boy slipped his hand from his mom's and toddled up to him. There the boy hunched down to watch him play, while the boy's delighted mother filmed her child's antics with her phone. The child was wrapped up in a blue cobalt snowsuit and wore a woolly hat and thick mittens. He bent his little legs so that his body moved up and down to the beat. His arms he jerked about above his head. A crowd began to gather. They clapped their hands as much in time to the boy's dance moves as to Seosamh's drum playing.

"Here, love," the toddler's mum said to her child. "Give this to the man."

The small boy took the two-euro coin from his mom in two hands. His first attempt at dropping it into Seosamh's cup landed it on the ground. The child doubled his body over but had great difficulty picking the coin up again. An old man stooped down and retrieved the coin. He handed it the boy with a grandfatherly smile. The boy made a yip of joy, jumped off the ground, and dropped it into Seosamh's paper cup.

"Thanks, son," he said. And he nodded at the old man. "Thank you, sir."

Seosamh continued to play on, his makeshift drumkit the subject of interest from some of the crowd and something to scoff at from others. But when the light-headedness returned, he took a break. Too long a break. The Arctic weather grew fiercer still. Falling snowflakes swirled around the streetlamps. And the freshly fallen snow crunched under footsteps.

So cold had it become, Seosamh could no longer play the pots and the pan he used as drums. He put down his wooden spoon drumsticks and blew into his hands.

"Happy Christmas," he said to a well-dressed young lady with a phone before her face. "I'm trying to get a room in a hostel before Santa comes tonight." This was one of his tapping lines.

Her eyes flicked from her phone as she walked on.

Seosamh eased himself off the ground, his back pressed against a lamppost. But his legs wouldn't work too well. So, he slid his back down the lamppost and into a seated position again.

He awoke from a slumber he didn't realise he'd fallen into. Inside his head a freezing headache. He clamped the heels of his hands to his temples.

Nearby, a bearded busker announced his last song and started into one Seosamh's mother used to sing back in the long ago. He could still hear his mother explaining to him and his sister how the song tells of a young boy who was summoned by the Magi to the Nativity of Christ, and how the little drummer boy was too poor to get the Christ child a gift, so he instead played his drums for him.

Seosamh buried his head in his chest and silently wept through the song and the applause. Finally, he looked up when he heard the tinkle of coins in his paper cup.

"Happy Christmas, bro," the bearded busker said.

With humility, the busker admitted, yes, when Seosamh asked him. He was the one who had left him the coffee earlier. And he added that he had cashed in Seosamh's bottles for him.

"Didn't want you to get to the inn and find it closed," the busker said. "It being Christmas Eve and all." He winked at him. "Oh, and this is from me." He put a twenty euro note into Seosamh's hand, clapped him on the shoulder, then back waved as he pushed off.

With a fire in him ignited by the good will of the busker and the boy from earlier, Seosamh found the strength to pack up his kit, and get himself to a chipper on the way back to Meryem. An unwelcome shock awaited him when he arrived at their tent. Meryem lay beneath the duvet without moving. Seosamh uncovered her head and brought his lips to her face. Her flesh was as cold as the food they stored in their plastic container.

Without forethought or consideration, Seosamh left the tent and removed the loose boulders of the drystone wall at the section where he'd seen the farmer doing so when letting his animals out the graze on the commonage. He then returned to Meryem. And, resummoning a strength which belonged to the days when he worked the building sites in foreign parts, he lifted her from inside the tent. Cradling her in his arms, he carried her to the cowshed.

When he got her settled, he worked his way back to where he'd left the bag of fish and chips. Gone. A fox no doubt. A hungry fox had got them.

The farmer came upon them in the stable when he was putting away the donkey, the fawn-coloured cow and her surrogate lamb for the night. The dishevelled couple who had been camping on the waste ground outside his land. The woman lay on the hay in the feeding trough, while the man approached him, bowing, his hands joined in supplication.

He apologised for trespassing, and for removing the stones from the wall. He hoped he'd put them back properly. He told him his wife, Meryem, was due to give birth to their first child. And he begged the farmer to extend hospitality and let them stay for a bit. They would leave soon after the child was born.

"I am Seosamh," the man told him.

The farmer, a poor man like the travellers, understood their plight in a way that would have been alien to those of means. He bid them welcome.

He went to tie up the donkey and the cow, but the animals seemed fascinated by the woman lying in the trough. Seosamh reassured the farmer there was no need to and that the heat from the animals' breath was welcome.

This recalled for the farmer tales told of a few generations back of the byres, a living space shared by the small farmer and his few animals. This he recounted to Seosamh and Meryem, before leaving them to settle in for the night.

Just before bedtime, the farmer returned to the stable with some leftovers from his own dinner for his guests. And with hot milk for the mother and something stronger for Seosamh. On entering the stable he heard a baby's cry, and a strange awe came over him. He approached the mother and newborn and went to his knees.

About the author
Steve Wade's short story collection, *In Fields of Butterfly Flames and Other Stories* was published by Bridge House Publishing in 2020. His fiction has been published and anthologised in over seventy print publications. He has had stories shortlisted for the Francis McManus Short Story Competition and the Hennessy Award.

Star over Dartmoor

Sharon Keely

Toby wasn't in his room. I looked out to the back garden, expecting to see a sneaker protruding from our Retriever's doghouse. Instead, the bottom of a sleeping bag poked out. Check bed – pillow missing. My brain zapped. Had he spent the night outside?

Three weeks since we'd put Delia down and he hadn't stopped crying. Every morning he came downstairs, eyes red and puffy, refilled her water bowl, then went back to his room and closed the door to cry again. I was at my wits' end. Why hadn't I ended Delia's suffering while school was still in session? Not that Toby loved school, but at least it would've been a distraction. Except the dear old girl hadn't been ready then. She'd still been dragging herself onto the air mattress Toby inflated for the pair of them when she could no longer get up the stairs.

"Why don't we ask your friends around?" got "I don't have any. Delia was my only friend." Which might've been true. That we were mostly a street of empty-nesters didn't help. "Wouldn't Delia like us to get a puppy? Rescue a dog like we did her."

"No Mum. I never ever want to feel this sad again."

I'd shed tears too, and still did when I came across clumps of her golden hair. But I'd lost so many others in my life; Toby hadn't. How had I not heard him creep outside? I'd heavily relied on Delia barking when anything was amiss.

A head of shiny black hair attached to clippers appeared on the other side of the back hedge. Old Mrs. Starbridge's place must have gone to a family with kids. The lad looked to be around Toby's age. "Dad!" he yelled, "Dad! There's a body at the bottom of the other garden!"

I chuckled; should go out and disabuse the boy, but maybe this would embarrass Toby out of future sleep-outs. He couldn't be outside on frosty mornings, though those were a way off yet. But might his embarrassment thwart his chance at making a friend? Now there were two heads over the hedge. The man had to be the dad.

"Hello," he called, "hello… you in the doghouse… are you alright?"

No answer, no movement. "OK, I'm coming over…"

That did it. Toby's head crawled out. "I'm not hurt. I'm just sad."

"Why?"

"My dog died."

"Oh, I am so sorry," the dad said. "Dogs are very special. Our spirit guides…"

He spotted me at the kitchen window and smiled. I smiled back, put my finger to my lips, and stage-stepped backwards. He got it and went on talking to Toby as if he hadn't seen me. In due time, a second set of shears was produced and handed to Toby, who cut the hedge from our side in lockstep with the new boy.

They seemed to be getting along well, chatting when they felt like it, comfortably – I hoped – silent when they didn't. Sometimes Toby craned his neck to talk to someone else on the other side. A smaller child? When they were nearing the end of the hedge, I took a tray to the patio table.

"Boys, snack?" I called. "There's enough for three. Milk with cheese and tomato sandwiches."

"I'll ask my dad, thank you!" the new boy called and disappeared. I'd been going to say, hop over onto the bench, but it was just as well I didn't. Toby ran back to me and said, "They'll come through the side gate." When they did, one of the boys was in a wheelchair. Abad and Ratanji, twins. They sat around the table and tucked in.

The dad appeared over the hedge again. We introduced ourselves. "Thank you," I said.

"No, thank you," Farzan replied, "It is lovely for the boys to make new friends so fast. And so near."

Toby called out, "Mum, Abad says Delia and lots of other dogs will be reincarnated as an otter!"

Farzan smiled sheepishly. "It is what we believe," he said. "One thousand dogs are reincarnated as an otter."

"One otter?" I raised an eyebrow.

"Yes, otters are sacred."

"Oh dear, now Toby will be trying to find an otter to bring home…"

"Well, there is an otter sanctuary in Dartmoor."

"'No," I said, more sharply than I intended.

"No, no," he laughed. "I don't mean bring one home to live in your bathtub. But Toby could adopt one and sometimes send pocket money… The otter stays in Dartmoor."

"Oh, that's a thought."

The boys came in to watch a movie, Abad taking off his shoes first. We weren't that kind of household; thankfully his socks were black. As Toby refilled Delia's water bowl, Abad eyed photos on the mantelpiece. He picked up one of Toby in the Christmas pageant where he'd played – rather, stood still on stage as – one of the Three Wise Men. Abad giggled and handed the photo down to Ratanji. "You were one of the Magi – trying to look like us."

"What do you mean?" Toby asked.

"My people – Zoroastrians. We were the Magi."

"I thought you said you were Parsees?"

"Yes but our religion is Zoroastrian. Our priests are called Magi. The Three Wise Men were our priests, mystical priests. I like your cloak."

"Mum made that for me. I still have it."

"Did you like being a Magus?" Ratanji asked.

140

Toby looked a little insulted.

"One Magus, three Magi," Abad explained.

"Oh. Not really. Simon said the wise men told Herod about baby Jesus, and that's why Herod had all the little boys killed. All the boys under two years old."

"That is because they didn't know why Herod was asking. They thought he was excited to meet baby Jesus too."

"But I thought they had magical powers."

"Mystical, but not magical. They spent their time looking at the stars. They could read stars like no-one else. But they were not so good at reading people. They thought everyone meant well, like them."

"I'm not good at reading people either," Toby said matter-of-factly.

"I could teach you to read stars though," Ratanji said.

"Could you??" This was the most excited I'd seen Toby since Christmas, since Delia started her long decline. "Would I be able to read the stars to know when Delia is reborn?"

Ratanji cocked his head to one slide. "Yes I think so. I will ask my dad."

Farzan opined that when the dog star, Sirius in the constellation Canis Majoris, was directly over Dartmoor, Delia would come back.

The rest of the summer was passed with daily trouping of the boys in and out of our houses and, when the weather allowed, backyard camping in a tent large enough to accommodate Ratanji's wheelchair, preceded by hours looking at the stars through telescopes. A major project was the building of an observatory-grade telescope in the twins' back garden. Another was making two Magi cloaks like Toby's, with the twins' mum, Parichehr, and I helping. Toby still had his crying jags when we were alone together; a few times, I heard him crying in his sleep. He still filled Delia's water bowl every day.

In late September, Farzan drew me aside. "It is around sixty days since Delia passed to the other side, yes?"

"Yes, July twentieth," I said.

"And the otter sanctuary tells me pups will be born this week," Farzan winked.

"Ah hah," I said. "Is the dog star over Dartmoor?"

"Always," he laughed.

"I sense a train journey in our future," I said.

"Yes," Farzan replied. "But it will be a month before we are allowed to see the pups. We can get a train to Exeter and rent a car from there."

Toby's excitement made me as giddy as him. "What gifts do we bring, mum?"

"Well for gold, I think the rescue always needs money."

"We can go in our cloaks and ask the neighbours!" Abad said. Toby clapped his hands in delight. To whomever had taken my glum little boy and lit him from within like this, I was eternally grateful. But of course, I knew who.

"And frankincense and myrrh?"

"That's a tricky one. Frankincense smelled nice; otters are supposed to be a bit stinky. Maybe hand lotion for the people who work there?"

"And myrrh?"

I was stumped on that one. "Could have been used as an ointment," Parichehr concluded.

She called Dartmoor; they gave her the name of a cream used for otters' fungal infections.

And so it came to pass that three boys in Magi cloaks entered the otter sanctuary bearing gifts on a Saturday morning, ahead of the scheduled opening time. Farzan had arranged a special viewing of the pups for them. Their wonder was contagious. We gasped and shed tears together. The mother lifted one squeaking pup up between her paws. Toby, sure she was showing it to him, sank to his knees and pressed his face to the glass. "Delia," he sobbed, "Delia. I've missed you so much…"

He fell asleep on the way back, his head in my lap, only waking when the train slowed outside Reading.

"Happy?" I asked. He nodded sleepily. "I hated thinking she was never coming back. I'm going to send all my pocket money to her. And see her as often as we can."

After a while he said, "Mum? Can we still get a new puppy? Now I know Delia is okay?"

Hallelujah, I thought.

"Of course, darling."

"'And mum, let's call him…"

Oh no. We would definitely have to come up with another name.

About the author
Sharon Keely grew up in Ireland, and wandered a bit, landing for extended periods in the U.K., Australia and the U.S., always heading straight to the bookstores.

Stories in *CafeLit*, *Book of Matches*, *The Wells Street Journal*, *Adelaide Lit*, *Scrimshaw*, *Audemus*. Poems in online publications.

The Census

John Walker

It was just after sunset on a wintry December day. He looked so tired as she brought the glass of wine he had ordered. "You've had a long day?" she asked with a bright and winsome smile.

"You could say that," he replied, firmly placing his clipboard on the table. He sipped on the wine and asked, "Do you work here?"

She replied, "Well, sort of – my parents own the pub, and I make the beds in the guest rooms above, scrub the floors, serve down here behind the bar – anything that needs doing really – my name's Rebecca. What brings you here?"

He looked at her – she was an attractive girl, maybe sixteen years old, with long black hair. He could check – he had all the files! "Casual work with the Stats Bureau," he said, "We've booked out most of the rooms here – we're doing the Census. My boss and his wife are in your 'Executive Suite' – he's from Rome, as you can imagine. It's OK for the bigwigs – I've had to leave my parents back there and check into your cheapest room!"

"Aaah, that explains the fantastic bookings for all our hotel rooms! It's not unusual for us to be half-empty in winter, but my parents are ecstatic over the extra business, and we're under so much pressure we had to make room in the shed for one poor young couple! We gave them blankets and made them comfortable, but that shed's used as a stable – the woman actually gave birth two nights ago – a donkey and two sheep for midwife and nurses! But it apparently went well – they have a baby boy! Called him Jesus, apparently."

He said, "I should introduce myself – I'll have to update

their form to take account of the baby! I'm Marcus – my job involves going door to door around the town noting how many people live there, their ages and gender, and how many rooms they have. Most of the houses here are single occupancy, so yours is a bit different. Lots of people have come here specifically for the Census, because it's compiled on a "place-of-birth" basis. It's a schemozzle, really – imagine what it's like for families who've moved from town to town – maybe they were born here but their kids could have been born in Nazareth or Haifa, or anywhere! That's why your rooms are full – and why they're making do in the shed – Bethlehem was quite a growth centre a few years ago! I have to get the details of all the people staying here tonight.

"Hi Marcus – well – you're welcome to Bethlehem!" she said. She noticed his mediterranean complexion and fine Roman nose, and his name, of course suggesting some Italian ancestry – maybe just a couple of years older than her. She continued, "It's been a weird week – firstly, that strange star you could still see in broad daylight, then we had the rush of visitors – and weirdest of all – three obviously obscenely rich guys arrived on camels! Can you believe it – they'd ridden hundreds of miles just wanting to see the baby – some prediction linked to that star – they reckoned he is somehow special apparently! They parked their camels outside and attracted quite a crowd! Even the camels' saddles were covered in gold and jewels!

"They brought him special presents – frankincense and myrrh, whatever they are! How inappropriate for a baby – they haven't the faintest clue how ordinary people live! What's wrong with nappies and swaddling clothes? The whole situation was absurd – here they are, these guys, dripping with jewellery and with crowns on their heads, on their knees in front of a manger mumbling homage to a new-born baby, while the baby's astonished parents looked on! But they did bring gold as well – and a fair bit of it I'm told – apparently the father is a carpenter in Nazareth – that will set him up in business for life! Good luck to him, I say!"

"Well," said Marcus, "you could be a young mother before too many years – what would you want as a present for your new-born?"

Rebecca's face lit up, and she hurried off – "Don't go away – I'll be back!" She returned a few minutes later with two more glasses of the very best wine they had, together with some delicious-looking nibbles – "On the house," she said – and a small furry toy.

"A Teddy Bear! I haven't seen one of those for years!" said Marcus. "I had one of those when my parents worked for the Colosseum in Rome. The real ones are not as nearly cute as this little guy – they would rip you to pieces at the drop of a hat!"

"This one was mine when I was little – I took him with me everywhere we went!," Rebecca replied – "I've never seen a real one, but I'd like to – from a respectable distance, maybe! I bet the baby would love him, and it would be a nice gesture from us."

Marcus expertly ripped two pages from his clipboard and, with some clear expertise in origami – something exceedingly rare in those days of the Roman Empire – skilfully turned them into gift wrapping, saying, "How about I write 'Happy Birthday, Jesus, from Marcus and Rebecca'?"

Rebecca quickly warmed to this idea – "Let's take it round to them – it would make us sort-of honorary godparents! What if those weird camel guys really knew their stuff, and this kid's something special? He'll grow up in Nazareth, with his teddy bear, and his parents would tell him where he came from, and all the weird things that happened at the time. And Teddy would remind them of us – how sweet!" They sipped their wines, ate their nibbles and exchanged a few deeply meaningful glances. "Are you planning to stay in Bethlehem long, or do you have to go back to Rome?" she asked, with that look in her eyes that suggested she was hoping for the right answer.

Marcus thought for a while and replied, "There's something very serendipitous about this whole weekend. The baby's sort-of crystallised it for me – let's go and give him the teddy bear, and then can you check how long I can keep that room? I like it here in Bethlehem…"

About the author

In real life John Walker is a retired criminologist, based in Sanctuary Point, NSW, Australia. Writing poetry started as a "pre-retirement" activity – preparing for life after work and keeping the brain cells active. It became a rather good way of passing time on long air journeys or while waiting for inspiration on a work project, or even going for a run in the bush! These days John wins poetry competitions, especially where a bit of humour is required. His first book, *The Loaded Doggerel*, is available via Echo Books: https://echobooks.com.au/our-books/the-loaded-doggerel.

Follow him on Facebook:
www.facebook.com/loadeddoggereller

The Family Legend

Allison Symes

My story has been passed down from father to son. I have just revealed it to my son now he has turned twelve. Our custom dictates things of importance are shared then and not before. I also consider it important enough to write this down. There must be properly kept records.

One day he will share it with his son and the family legend will be kept safe this way. Yes, I've written it down for you to see now but you will not know who my family are. I will not allow anyone to trace them.

There are those who would make us suffer for telling the truth about what we know. He always has been a controversial figure, you see. Always will be, we think. And while you think you have names for us, there is no evidence to support those thoughts. Do not presume. Do know I am telling you the truth here though. I am using the names you think you know for your convenience, that is all, and to stop confusion on your part.

It is also my belief if He wants you to see this story, He will ensure you see it in a language you understand.

Who am I? I am the son of one of the Magi who followed the special star to that stable in Bethlehem. I was twelve when he went. I wanted to go with him, of course. What boy of that age wouldn't want to go? It would have been the adventure of my life but it was ruled out by my parents.

I was fascinated by the tale because Father pointed out the star to me before he left. I've never seen a star that bright before or since. I doubt anyone will see anything like it again.

The journey was longer than Father and his friends anticipated. Neither had they expected to end up where they did. They clung to their belief they had gone to see a king though what sort of monarch ends up being born in a stable was beyond me. It still is, to be honest.

It took months for them to reach their destination and they were longer getting home, given they had to take a different route. News about Herod's atrocity reached us – the merchants are fabulous for spreading news – before Father and his friends returned. I conceded then my parents may have had a point in not allowing me to go.

When Father and his friends were told about it – my mother broke the news – they went so pale. Indeed, we thought the youngest was going to faint but he muttered something about how we should never ignore dreams. They're often trying to tell us something; it's up to us to be alert to that and to hearing His voice.

Naturally on sharing their story with us, they focused on the more positive aspects to their journey – the family in the stable, and how they presented gifts suitable for a king – gold and frankincense.

The youngest, the one you know as Caspar, was inspired to bring myrrh but could not say why. He just knew it was the right thing to take. The others assumed, rightly as it turned out, Caspar had been inspired by the Highest Authority of all to take it. What was not clear was the reason – the other two gifts are obvious.

We found out later, again thanks to the merchants, the family had to flee Herod, but Father was comforted by the thought that the gold would have bought a lot of unseeing eyes as the family went into Egypt. The frankincense too could be sold if needed. The man, Joseph, would have needed something for his family to survive on until he had his carpentry business up and running again.

So where do I come into all of this, other than to be told Father's story?

Only to say he wasn't the only one to make this journey

along with his friends. I went too, years later. Word had reached us of a special teacher and healer working in Judea. He'd known, thanks to the star, the baby was special as it heralded the birth of a king. It was a question of just how special this baby could be.

Father was an old man by this time but he wondered if this teacher could be the babe he had gone to see thirty-three years previously. So when word got out about the miracles and the man preaching with authority, so unlike the scribes and Pharisees, Father's instincts told him this had to be the same person.This king was to be different from the rest. Father and his friends all thought so. Kings come and go. Who else has a special star emerge?

Father then wondered how it would be possible to find out. Mother and I knew he would not be at ease until he did know.

I said I would go. It pleased Father but not my mother. It turned out she and the other wives had wanted to go with their husbands all those years ago too but the men wouldn't hear of it. I know how they felt, of course; I sympathised. It didn't make the ladies feel any better. To be fair, when my mother tried to console me for not going, that didn't work either.

So I went. I joined a group of merchants. I have a gift for languages and proved useful to them on the way. They were sorry when I parted company with them.

Unlike Father, I vowed not to go near any royal palace. I believe there might be a saying somewhere about not being bitten twice. If not, there should be. Unlike Father, I had no star to guide me. But he had drawn maps. He had a fabulous artistic talent. It made such a difference to my trip; I am sure it took some time off the journey time (days certainly).

What did I find out when I did get to Bethlehem? Well, I wanted to see the stable. It was still there when I went but it will not last forever. I did talk to the innkeeper and his wife. They were still running the inn, though they are getting on in years. They remembered that birth only too well and were pleased to see me. I was relieved. You can never know what welcome a foreigner will receive. They told me where to find the preacher and healer. So I headed towards Capernaum and I saw Him.

Father had drawn a picture of the baby he met all those years ago but, more importantly, what he thought the child would look like as a grown man. He drew two images of the latter in fact – one with Him with a beard and one without. Father claimed he felt inspired by the Higher Power to draw as he did. All I know is I recognised the Man immediately. I smiled. I could return home and let Father know.

But then things went wrong. The authorities were not happy with the preaching and healing He was doing. I found this out from those locals who were willing to talk to me. There were not many but there were some. I overheard a lot too as merchants get everywhere and, on setting up their stalls, the first thing they do is gossip. I also met up with some of those I had travelled with who were only too pleased to tell me what they had heard. The latter told me the authorities arrested Him.

I then went to Jerusalem. I had to see what happened next. Also, I knew Father and his friends would want to know.

I was in the crowd when He was sentenced. I stayed quiet as the mob around me bayed for His blood. To be honest, I was frightened. I also had no idea what I could do.

I was in the crowd when He was crucified. I watched from a distance as His friends put Him in a borrowed tomb.

And then I knew, I finally knew, what the myrrh was for.

Casper had been right. King and God and sacrifice. My father saw the King, believed in the divine revelation this Man was more than just human, and I saw the sacrifice.

Three days later, as I was preparing to head home, I heard strange stories about a resurrection. The authorities did try to cover that up but failed. Word spread fast. You are not going to hide a story like that, as, especially with the best will in the world, from what I saw of His friends none of them looked capable of inventing any fantastic tale.

I decided to take the Emmaus road to head home. Like Father and his friends all those years ago, I too went a different way home. Sometimes you just know a good idea when you hear it, and I hadn't needed a strange dream to get the message home either.

A little ahead of me on the road I saw two men engaged in earnest conversation with another Man. I recognised Him. He looked up and saw me. He smiled before resuming his discussion. I rode past them, lifting a hand in greeting, and bowed my head to Him. It seemed appropriate.

When I returned home, I found Father was ill and my mother told me Casper and the one you know as Balthazar were also not well. I told Father what I have just told you. I also told the others.

Casper died not long afterwards but he was smiling as I witnessed his passing and I was privileged to hear his last words.

"Now I know why I had to take the myrrh."

About the author

Allison Symes, who loves quirky fiction, is published by Chapeltown Books, CaféLit, and Bridge House Publishing. She writes for *Chandler's Ford Today* and *Writers' Narrative*.

Website: https://allisonsymescollectedworks.com
Books: http://author.to/AllisonSymesAuthorCent
YouTube: www.youtube.com/@allisonsymes

Her flash fiction collections are *From Light to Dark and Back Again* and *Tripping the Flash Fantastic*.

The Four Wise Men

Ian Inglis

I like letters. Letters and cards. I always have. For as long as I can remember. As a child, there was something exciting about looking out of the window for a first glimpse of the postman, or racing down the stairs when I heard the snap of the letter-box and the soft thud of the mail as it fell to the floor. Coming at roughly the same time every morning (sometimes even twice a day) there was a ritual element to each delivery that helped to structure my day. Oh, I know emails and texts are quicker, more immediate, more efficient – but they provoke none of the thrill of anticipation that I used to feel. People tell me I'm stuck in the past, that I need to move with the times, that I'm an incurable romantic. I'm sure they're right. But for people of my generation, many of our most memorable and important communications – happy and sad – were delivered that way: examination results, offers from university, postal orders from distant aunts and uncles, holiday postcards, letters from penpals, rejections and invitations, birthday cards, messages of sympathy, expressions of support, love letters…

The only letters I have today – the only ones I've kept – are those that Anna and I wrote to each other, after my family moved from York to London. It was more than fifty years ago now, and predictably enough, most of them – two or three a week at times – were about how much we were missing each other. I have all of them, arranged in chronological order in a large box. On several occasions I was on the point of destroying them. In those days, I was young and foolish, always looking for the dramatic gesture, the ostentatious sacrifice, the impassioned course of action that I fondly imagined would transform me into a heroic, tragic figure who would haunt the consciences of all who knew me. Fortunately, I came to my senses, and chose to store them away, rather than burn them. I don't often read them, but knowing that they still exist, having them close to me, is a source of comfort, something to jog my memory as I get older.

We met on our first morning at what my parents called "the big school." We'd both passed the 11-plus and had been offered places at that rare thing, a mixed grammar school, where the teachers (most of whom wore gowns, and were fierce disciplinarians) wasted no time in telling us that we represented the top ten per cent of the country's pupils, and should behave accordingly. I remember Anna was far less impressed than I was.

"We don't have to take them seriously," she said, as we shuffled from one classroom to another.

"Who?"

"Who do you think? Most of them are only here because there was a shortage of qualified teachers after the war."

"How do you know?"

"My father told me."

"And how does he know?"

"He's a teacher himself!"

We both laughed, and from then on, we were inseparable companions. We joined the same school clubs and societies (the Literary & Debating Society, the Chess Club, the Drama Society), we signed up for the same field trips (Jodrell Bank, Snowdon, Hadrian's Wall), we chose to study the same optional subjects (French rather than German, Music rather than Chemistry). We'd often walk to and from school together, discussing our homework, comparing our approaches.

"You should try something different," I said, as we talked about our forthcoming half-term essay on *Romeo And Juliet*.

"In what way?"

"Well," I continued, "everyone will write that it's the world's greatest love story, two star-crossed lovers united in death, a tragic romance, and so on."

"Isn't it?"

"It might be, yes. But you could look at it from another point of view – that Romeo and Juliet are two spoiled, selfish, immature adolescents. They're only thirteen or fourteen – can you really be in love at that age? Isn't it just a teenage crush? After all, at the start of the play, Romeo's telling everyone how much he loves Rosaline. His gang are constantly boasting and threatening, getting into street brawls. Don't forget, he kills two people, Tybalt and Paris. And they get married the day after they've met! That's hardly sensible, is it? And then they commit suicide without a moment's thought for their friends, their families, their parents. They're not what I'd call likeable characters. It's a tragedy, yes, but I'm not sure it's a love story."

"Is that what you're going to argue in your essay?"

"Yes."

"Then I will too!"

When my parents made their long-planned and much-delayed move to London, we told each other that it was not an end to our friendship, but a mere interruption. In fact, I settled in to my new school in the suburbs surprisingly quickly, and made many friends. Without a telephone in either of our houses, the regular flow of letters between us soon became a routine part of my life. Apart from our protestations of undying affection and loyalty, what else did we write about? Art (there were so many galleries and exhibitions in London that I wanted to tell her about), poetry (she introduced me to Walt Whitman, I introduced her to Pablo Neruda), the theatre (my outings to the West End, and hers to the theatres in York) and the cinema (we'd arrange to see the same movie on the same evening in our different cities, and pretend we'd watched it together).

But most of all, we wrote about the music. Our music. As the decade unfolded, all the colour and brightness and energy and optimism of those years seemed to coalesce around its sounds... the sounds of the sixties. Suddenly, the Alma Cogans, the Cliff Richards, the Frankie Vaughans were revealed for what we had always secretly known they were: bland, superficial performers with little or no real talent; the songs they sang predictable, sentimental, insipid ballads; the radio and TV shows on which they appeared embarrassing, slightly ludicrous, and hopelessly old-fashioned.

Our own musical revolution – hers and mine – began, as it did for so many people, with the Beatles. Here's one of the very first letters she wrote to me in London. It was in the Autumn of 1962:

I was listening to Radio Luxembourg last night and I heard a new record by a group called the Beetles. I think it's called Love Me Do. *It's really good, you should listen out for it.*

A week or so later, I was able to reply:

That group you mentioned. It's Beatles not Beetles. I saw them on TV. Four of them. They're from Liverpool. They're great. Strange hairstyles. They sang both sides of their single, "Love Me Do" and "PS I Love You", and then they were interviewed. The leader is called John Lennon... he's the one who stands with his leg apart. He's really funny and doesn't care what he says! He's my favourite.

And when their first album *Please Please Me* was released a few months later, we were astonished and delighted to see that one of the tracks was called "Anna". This was no coincidence! It was a sign! It had to be! That was the start. For the next few years, on my visits back to York, Anna's trips down to London, and in our letters and postcards, we used the Beatles and their music as touchstones for the ups and downs of our friendship. We looked for them in vain, wherever we went – in Carnaby Street, in the Kings Road, in Portobello Road Market. We watched them, in glorious black-and-white, on *Ready Steady Go!*, on *Top Of The Pops*, on *Thank Your Lucky Stars*, on a special edition of *Juke Box Jury*. We tuned in to the Light Programme to hear them on *Saturday Club* and *Easy Beat*. We read the monthly fan-club magazine, and learned of their early years in Liverpool and Hamburg. We became aware of Brian Epstein, George Martin, Pete Best, Stuart Sutcliffe. We scoured the pages of the *New Musical Express* each week for news about the group. We bought the records, listened to the songs, danced to the music, analysed the lyrics.

"Is that about drugs?" I asked her, as we listened for the first time to "I Want To Hold Your Hand".

"Where? What do you mean?"

"Here… where they sing 'When I touch you I feel happy inside; it's such a feeling that my love, I get high'. Getting high… isn't that to do with drugs?"

When she stopped laughing, she explained.

"It's not 'my love, I get high'. It's 'my love I can't hide'. Listen again."

Our letters were filled with comments about each new single, each new album, their television appearances on

157

Sunday Night At The London Palladium and the *Royal Variety Show*, the worldwide spread of Beatlemania, their spectacular success in the USA, the two movies, the row over their MBEs. We loved the fact that they were not remote superstars living in secluded mansions like Elvis Presley, or members of an international jet-set like Frank Sinatra, but everyday youngsters whose lives weren't too different from ours. And as they changed, we changed with them. When much of the adult world attacked them after John Lennon's observation that the Beatles were more popular than Jesus, we knew exactly what he meant; when he incurred the wrath of the British establishment for returning his MBE, we rejoiced in his integrity; when he began his long relationship with Yoko Ono, we wished him well. When Paul McCartney admitted that he'd taken LSD, we applauded him for his honesty. When George Harrison fell under the spell of the Maharishi Mahesh Yogi and persuaded the group to study transcendental meditation in Rishikesh in Northern India, we admired his thirst for knowledge. When Ringo Starr appeared in *Candy* and *The Magic Christian* alongside the likes of Marlon Brando, Richard Burton, Peter Sellers, John Huston and Richard Attenborough, we didn't question his acting ambitions. They could do no wrong in our eyes.

Best of all, we saw them! And not once, but twice. When they appeared at the Rialto in York, in March 1963, Anna managed to get hold of two tickets, and my parents – much to my amazement – allowed me to take a couple of days off school to travel up from London for the show. I spent most of the train journey trying to comb my hair forward in a weak imitation of their haircuts. There were only three Beatles that night. John Lennon was missing with a heavy cold and although his absence was a disappointment at the time, I rarely miss the opportunity to bewilder people when I tell them I saw the Beatles when they were a trio. And then the following year, we saw all four of them when my parents took us along to see their Christmas show at the Hammersmith Odeon in 1964. On both occasions, the screaming all but blocked out the sound of the music, but the excitement of those nights was unforgettable. My only regret is that I didn't save the tickets – not for their considerable financial value, but as a concrete souvenir of their performances.

There were lots of other groups we liked too: the Kinks, the Hollies, the Animals, the Small Faces, the Rolling Stones, the Searchers. And there were others we didn't like: the Dave Clark Five, Herman's Hermits, Freddie & the Dreamers, the Bachelors. But no-one ever came close to the Beatles. No-one ever could. No-one ever has. No-one ever will. We knew it the first time we heard them. They and their music were special. There was a joyousness, an exuberance, about their songs that was impossible to ignore, impossible to contain: even the sad songs – "Misery", "I'm A Loser", "Help", "I'm Down", "No Reply" – had a playful, exhilarating quality that masked their gloomy lyrics. And their presence quickly went far beyond the musical. Newspaper articles praised their movies and compared them to the Marx Brothers. Academics searched for psychological and sociological explanations for Beatlemania. Their social and cultural impact was discussed on late-night TV programmes. Politicians courted them. Their arrivals and departures from airports around the globe – even their press conferences – became events in themselves. In everything they did, they overwhelmed us. They overwhelmed the world. They became an integral part of who we were. Their sense of fun was irresistible. Somewhere between court jesters and public intellectuals, they commented on topics that previous pop stars studiously avoided – the Vietnam War, drugs, religion, the evils of racism, the status of marriage. We listened to them. We learned from them. They became our guides, our role models, our interpreters, our mentors. That's when we coined our own private name for them: the four wise men. In almost every letter we wrote to each other, John, Paul, George and Ringo were there, in some form or other.

Ironically, one of the few letters in which they were not present is the one I think of most often – the last one, the one Anna sent me after we'd finished our A levels. We'd agreed to apply to the same universities and had both been offered places at Bristol to study English Literature. We'd been planning it, looking forward to it, for months. And then she wrote to tell me she'd changed her mind. She was going to Durham instead:

You've been my closest friend for as long as I can remember. But think it's time to move on. University gives us that chance. We can meet new people, discover new things about ourselves. Isn't that what growing up is all about? We shouldn't simply carry on in the same way, doing what we've always done. I know you'll be upset, but I also know that I'm right. And so will you.

I was upset. More than upset – heartbroken. The letter arrived on a Saturday morning. I was playing *Revolver* for the hundredth time on my family's new stereo system and was listening to "Eleanor Rigby" while I read what she'd written. I suddenly saw myself as one of the lonely people Paul McCartney was singing about. I was too shattered to reply. I didn't. I couldn't. There was nothing I could say. For weeks, I couldn't bear to hear the song, and even today, beautiful as it is, it's probably my least favourite of all their records. Gradually, I came to accept her decision, to understand that she was right, although it took me some time to realise it, and for a while I hated her. But I went to

Bristol, fell in love with the city and, just as she predicted, we both moved on and did things we could never have done if we'd stayed together.

How many times have we seen each other since then? Not many. The weddings of a few mutual friends, an ill-advised school reunion, a chance encounter in Terminal 5 of Heathrow Airport. I remember she phoned me when John Lennon was murdered (we were both in tears) and again when George Harrison died. I know that on both occasions we promised to keep in touch. But we didn't. Our relationship/romance/attachment – whatever you want to call it – was simple and innocent and carefree, and I suppose that's the image of us that I like to preserve, even though it ended more than fifty years ago: had we stayed together, the mundane reality of two elderly people quietly sharing a pot of tea and doing what elderly people do – losing their hair, mending a fuse, knitting a sweater, wasting away – wouldn't have had quite the same attraction!

But she's never been far from my thoughts. The Beatles themselves have seen to that. Each new documentary, re-release, biography, every honour given to Paul or Ringo, each anniversary of this or that event in their career takes me back to her, to us. I'm not quite sure why. Other people have played far more significant roles in my life – after all, I've been married three times, and have five children and seven grandchildren. So, what is it? Perhaps it's a combination of things – the people Anna and I were, the excitement of the sixties, the passion of youth, the seductive power of nostalgia. Most of all, the perennial presence of the Beatles: just as we knew then and the world knows now, their music will last forever.

And there's something else about their music, something that I like to think makes for an odd personal

161

connection. In the first letters we sent to each other, we talked about "Love Me Do" and "PS I Love You". When I listen to the opening lines of "PS I Love You" – *As I write this letter, send my love to you* – I realise that's exactly what we were doing – writing letters and sending our love to each other. And while we were writing letters about the Beatles' songs, the Beatles were writing songs about letters. Because it wasn't just "PS I Love You". There were others too: addressing a letter in "Paperback Writer", waiting for the mail to arrive in "Please Mister Postman", sending a love letter in "All My Loving", a birthday message in "Birthday", an invitation in "Carry That Weight", a farewell note in "She's Leaving Home", a Valentine card in "When I'm Sixty-Four", postcards in "Two Of Us". Songs and letters, letters and songs. Written at the same time, writing at the same time. Anna, me, and the Beatles.

"What do you think we'd say to them if we ever met them?" she asked me once.

"I'd say thank you. I'd thank them for all the happiness their music has given me. What about you?"

"I think I'd ask them what it's like being a Beatle every day of their lives. How do they cope? How do they manage it? Do they ever regret it? Do they ever wish for a normal life?"

Several weeks ago, I heard that Anna had died. My career in the film industry had taken me out of the country for long periods and I hadn't seen her for many years, but I knew she'd been in poor health for a while, and her death wasn't unexpected. In many ways, her life had been surprisingly quiet, conservative, conventional. After her three years in Durham, she'd returned to York, followed her father's example by becoming a teacher, married a solicitor (I was invited to the wedding but didn't attend), and became a keen cyclist and rower. Her daughter wrote to tell me: *a malignant neoplasm of the bronchus and lung.* Lung cancer – although she'd never smoked in her life. I caught the train to the funeral, in a woodland setting on the outskirts of York. A simple, humanist service. No hymns. "In My Life" and "All You Need Is Love" played over the crematorium's sound system; Pablo Neruda's "If You Forget Me" read by one of her grand-daughters; a performance of Debussy's "Clair de Lune" by her niece.

As the mourners began to file out, I stood in front of the condolences book for some time, wondering, what, if anything, I could add to the many messages of sympathy and loss. I saw it as an opportunity to finally reply to her last letter, but I had no idea what to write. A simple phrase? A quotation? A line from a Beatles song? A few brief words or a lengthier tribute? In the end, I wrote nothing. There was still nothing I could say. I turned and walked away, avoiding the glances of those members of Anna's family who might have recognized me, and made my way to the station and the 6.30 train to London. Exhausted by the day's events and the emotions that had accompanied them I fell asleep, wondering if the young boy I had been then might recognize anything of himself in the old man I am now. I woke with a start an hour later as we pulled out of Doncaster, and picked up a discarded copy of the evening newspaper from the seat next to mine. As the train gathered speed, I read that a "new" Beatles single was about to be released, sixty-one years after "Love Me Do". It had been assembled from a scratchy, unfinished tape-recording made by John Lennon in the 1970s, and refined by studio advances which had allowed contributions from the other three Beatles. I'm not sure I wholly approve of the artificial reconstruction of discarded tracks, but I read on, intrigued by the details of the AI extraction technology. I stared at

163

the song's title for several seconds, and felt the past hurtling through the years to intertwine with the present. Anna and me: then and now. And our four wise men, the Beatles: "Now and Then".

About the author
Ian Inglis was born in Stoke-on-Trent and now lives in Newcastle upon Tyne. His stories have appeared in numerous anthologies and literary magazines in the UK and US, and his debut collection of short fiction *The Day Chuck Berry Died* was published by Bridge House in 2023.

The Gift of Common Ground

Anne Meale

Rectangular obsidian tiles hovered in mid-air as the game was halted, the players pausing briefly to watch us decide whether or not we were stopping at the bar to eat. They would have witnessed a family of three: frazzled, sweating parents and daughter on the brink of adolescence, the pre-teen default setting of disinterest already threatening to reside for the next few years. To be fair to her current temperament, we had meandered around this Catalonian town for longer than had been originally planned – lunch was encroaching on to afternoon tea, hangryness was indeed a thing.

We had deliberately chosen not to return to the hotel via the main promenade; it was, in the main, unsheltered from a flaring July sun, and no one would have suspected us of being anything but Scottish with our tell-tale argent skin. If further clues to our heritage had been sought, one glance at my daughter's paprika curls would have terminated that trail immediately.

Stomachs had reached the point of growling nausea; anywhere serving fare that wasn't priced at a gullible tourist tariff and wouldn't be greeted by the wrinkled-up nose of a fussy twelve-year-old would hit the spot. The unassuming tavern on the passageway between resort and residential area was looking favourable.

I popped my head inside the most sombre of premises and asked in basic Catalan if lunch was still being served. A curt nod led us to procure an outside table, sheltered under a canvas awning, the sun blocked by the towering holiday apartments across the road. There was one remaining, next to three venerable customers, who did little to disguise their curious staring, and my daughter pounced on her seat of choice, grateful to be resting aching feet, weary from an extended excursion in flimsy sandals.

Without thinking, we had arranged our chairs into a circle, and after doing so, discerned how all the other patrons faced the street, even the line of men engrossed in playing dominoes over canyas of beer. My daughter stayed put, however, her back to the road and the advancing sun's rays, opposite her parents, who tried to blend in at what was plainly a local bar for local people.

We were fairly muted as we awaited our pizzas; we'd explored extensively that day, and had we not become ravenous, would have enjoyed a siesta back in our hotel room to recuperate from the accumulated kilometres. My partner and I were content to watch the fluctuations of the avenue's activity in lazy contemplation: the parakeets frequenting the trees that encroached pavements and tore up the tiles with their errant roots, the Mossos d'Esquadra patrolling in their police cars, ready to act on the slightest hint of a fracas or the appearance of an illegal street vendor, wizened and stooped old women shuffling past with shopping trolleys packed with market produce and the sass of advanced years.

Without meaning to, I became attuned to the conversation next to me, the dominoes trio holding court on their local town hall and all its failings. I loved the sound of spoken Catalan; I could not understand why an Andalusian friend had described it as akin to barking dogs – to him it was guttural, a non-language. To me, it was a waterfall of syllables, a stream rippling over pebbles and bathing my senses with a softness that ached to be touched. Over time, I had come to prefer its harmonies to those of its Castilian associate, although it was natural to feel so in a town where one was steeped in its historical prose.

I was able to speak some of it, having taken lessons online for the best part of a year. Being a natural linguist, I could understand more than I could voice, there being some similarities to Spanish, French and Italian with a twist of Latin, and the old men were parlaying at a surprisingly slow rate – not the usual situation in this part of the world, I had hitherto found.

The next subject of their disapproval was their government. Understandable – wasn't it the done thing to lambast one's administration? Whether you'd voted them in or not was inconsequential. Those senescent citizens were getting stuck into their leaders with tongues of serpents, passion causing the words to accelerate into elongated sentences that I struggled to follow, but which spewed distaste. I caught some vocabulary I knew:

corruptes – corrupt
feble – weak
fora de contacte – out of touch

I compared my situation with theirs. Little difference, probably. Leadership in Catalonia was an emotive subject, understandable since the Civil War with its ensuing dictatorship and repercussions. There was an ardent desire in some quarters for independence – not an out and out one-sidedness, but enough to keep the topic high on the agenda. I suspected my fellow consumers would have had plenty to criticise whichever way the referendums swung.

The silver magi segued on to the topic of the Church; from the way the words were spat from lips, there were clearly no love from any of them for the institution. They were of the age that would have lived under Franco's regime and witnessed its persecutions, no matter which faction they had supported. The Church had done itself no favours siding with the Nationalists: the burning down of their buildings was testimony to that. Feelings and memories ran deep, because families throughout Spain had been torn apart and discarded like broken dolls.

A blur that turned out to be a speeding Guardia Civil car dashed up the street, siren shrieking enough to unsettle the parakeets: they flew up from their canopied shelters in puffs of green feathers. My nearest neighbour gave a derisory snort, followed by a word, had I not already known was a profanity, I would have guessed by the tone in which it was expressed. The jeer was echoed by the man in the middle, then the one on his left, with accompanying *tsk*s thrown in for good measure. I barely contained my beaming grin as I listened to the forthcoming critique of the national police force; these townsmen had plenty of ideas how they could be bettered, and ended their lecture with a triad of guffaws after the middle one's declaration that they couldn't catch a cold.

As if to not be outdone by the pinnacle of Spanish law enforcement, we were treated to the presence of two vehicles belonging to the Mossos d'Esquadra, the police unit under the authority of the Catalonia government, crawling past like tricoloured tortoises under metal shells. They were deemed of no use either.

Over several slices of pizza, many things proved unworthy of my neighbours' admiration; a list was compiled, including everything from rowdy tourists to incorrectly made *pa amb tomaquet*, from the education system to the province's lengthening drought conditions. A dominoes game ended, another begun. Small receptacles of vermut arrived and were quaffed as though they were spring water. These princes of the town paused in their musings to enjoy a blast of heat crossing their furrowed faces, two of them donning hats to protect vulnerable scalps as the sun inveigled its way into a gap between two buildings. The only sounds in our vicinity were squeaks and high-pitched melodies from the displaced birds now returned to their leafy abodes.

I reached out to fetch sunglasses from my bag and locked eyes with the gentleman on my left, who was pulling down his cap's peak to shield inquisitive nut-brown eyes from the vivid brightness. I smiled and addressed him in hesitant Catalan.

"It is a sunny day, today."

I was regarded with a look of shock, not unkindly, but surprised, nonetheless.

I continued. "We are not used to this weather in Scotland!"

His weathered face morphed slowly into a smile, which changed to a grin then a loud roar of laughter that echoed throughout the backstreets, the notes bouncing off the walls and permeating the balmy air with decades of spirit.

"The Scottish girl, she speaks Catalan!" he shrieked to his friends, who were not as bemused as my fifty-year-old self being referred to as a "girl". Delighted, I'm sure. He turned to me and gripped both my hands, pulling me into an embrace and then planted an exuberant kiss on each cheek.

His compatriots followed suit, even though I protested I was just a beginner, but their enthusiasm was infectious, and I found myself giddy with pleasure. Despite my limited vocabulary and confidence, their zeal encouraged me to prolong our conversation – the phrase, "what is the Catalan word for…" was going to be engraved on my tombstone after this.

The triumvirate were agog at my reasoning for learning their native tongue; they could not understand why a tourist from my country would even bother. I'd always loved learning languages; my school qualifications included three of them and I'd learned two more just for fun – pandemics will do that to you. My Spanish was fairly decent, but I'd wanted to try learning what I'd initially thought to be a variant of this, being that we were frequent visitors to this part of Spain. I promptly ascertained that it was a language all of its own. Catalan had me intrigued, dazzled, and thoroughly loved up.

I had enough of it to explain that we hailed from the north east of Scotland.

"We too are north east!"

From a place known for fish.

"Us too!"

The capless gentleman stated that we had much in common, the Catalans and the Scots: that we had little time for our government and that independence was the way. Although I was somewhat in agreement with the first, I chose not to reveal that I wasn't a supporter of the second – I'd heard them let rip on subjects they didn't agree with; I didn't want to become the next bullet point on their list. So, I smiled, nodded, asked for lots of repetition, *lentament, si us plau, slowly please* and introduced my family, who were greeted fervently and genially.

My attempts at joining in with conversation were humble and flawed, but met with craggy countenances that shone with delight and awe – I was only corrected when I asked for help – and I felt drunk on their appreciation of my appreciation: for their language, for their culture, for their land. Every so often that nonplussed phrase rang out: *The Scottish girl speaks Catalan!* Ah, the word "girl" again. I'd found my tribe.

We spoke of each other's countries. The townsmen's initial tone of pessimism, once I'd greeted them in their language had changed to one of jubilation, their pleasure at discovering a very pale Scot who had seen the value of their speech and was making the effort to acquire and use it.

How fascinating that different languages could rent a

world apart, yet here, outside an unassuming bar in a Catalonian resort, we were enhancing one over slices of pizza, dominoes and friendship.

My partner addressed me in hushed tones. "You're loving this, aren't you?" And I was. I truly was. I felt illuminated.

We passed the time, teachers and pupil from different generations, countries, tongues – but I was made to feel like a long-lost friend, their acceptance a heavy cloak around my shoulders drawing me in. I was almost reluctant to leave their company, but neither did I want to exclude my family, who had been sitting patiently, politely, letting me indulge myself in a meeting of minds. We got up to leave, and again, were enveloped in hugs all round and a farewell worthy of companions they had known all their lives. As we walked up the leafy street, I was aware that I was still beaming, that I was warmed.

I laughed at my partner's query. "Are you meeting your new cronies tomorrow, then?" I still wonder if he was half-serious.

I *was* tempted to swing past, on the off chance.

That one dialogue had bequeathed me so much. Three gifts: inclusion, confidence, joy. Joy to the world, one which should continue to be judged by domino-playing gentlemen in the backstreets, so as not to rest on its laurels, for to do so is dangerous. No administration should ever go uncriticised.

When the minutiae of memories from that holiday faded, the way this afternoon made me feel would linger, bringing butterflies to my belly and a smile to my face. I hoped those three men would remember the Scottish girl tripping through a hodgepodge of Catalan and Spanish, a quagmire of words – with little skill but vats of determination in its place; it was they who brought that out.

Everyone listening and learning. Common ground under an azure Catalonian sky.

About the author

Anne has written stories since childhood. She tackles most genres, but especially enjoys historical fiction and the research required for it. Anne lives in the North-East of Scotland with her family, is an ASN teacher, with an ambition to write full-time. She is currently querying her first novel and working on her second. Anne was the winner of the Burnham Book Festival Short Story Competition 2025.

The Lost Magus of Michigan

Rob Whaley

The sky split open, and Balthazar fell.

His body, wrapped in flowing silks of the East, crashed through a snow-laden pine and landed face-first in a frozen drift. The air was sharp and foreign, filled with the scent of pine and gasoline. Somewhere in the distance, wolves howled, or perhaps that was just the wind.

Balthazar groaned and rolled onto his back, staring up at the swirling grey sky. The Star of Bethlehem was gone. No desert sands, no caravans, no Melchior or Caspar. Only a frozen wasteland.

"Blessed Father," he whispered, breath curling in the frigid air. "I have made a wrong turn."

A voice crackled behind him. "Buddy, you all right?"

Balthazar sat up with a jolt, squinting at the figure before him – a man clad in thick boots, a Carhartt jacket, and a fur-lined Stormy Kromer cap. He held an ice fishing pole in one hand and a can of KBC beer in the other. Behind him sat a small shack with a wisp of smoke curling from a vent.

"Have I arrived in Bethlehem?" Balthazar asked. "I bear frankincense for the newborn King."

The man scratched his chin. "Bethlehem? Uh, nah, bud. You're in the U.P."

Balthazar blinked. "The U…P?"

"Upper Peninsula. Michigan. Cold as hell." The man peered at him. "You hit your head or somethin'?"

Balthazar stood, his silk robes stiffening in the cold. He clutched the clay jar of frankincense to his chest. "I must reach Bethlehem! Where is my camel?"

The man snorted. "Ain't seen no camels round here. Closest you'll get is a deer with an attitude."

"Then how does one travel?"

"Snowmobile's your best bet, but ain't nobody givin' theirs up for free. You got money?"

Balthazar hesitated, then reached into his pouch and pulled out a gold coin.

The man whistled. "Well, ain't that somethin'. Tell ya what: I know a guy who'll take ya south. Head to the gas station in town, ask for Big Vern. Tell him Tiny Lou sent ya."

Balthazar bowed. "You have my thanks, Prophet of the Ice."

Tiny Lou shrugged. "Yeah, okay. Want a pasty before ya go?"

Balthazar frowned. "A... pasty?"

"Meat pie. Warms ya up."

Balthazar accepted the steaming bundle and bit in cautiously. His eyes widened. "By the grace of the heavens, this is divine."

Tiny Lou grinned. "Yeah, they're pretty good."

The Journey to Frankenmuth

Balthazar's journey south was an exercise in confusion. While he understood the general meaning of words, much of the dialect and slang of these northern men baffled him.

His first attempt at snow travel ended abruptly when he was handed the reins of a snowmobile. The roaring machine took off faster than any camel he had ever commanded, sending him hurtling into a bank of powder. As he lay half-buried in snow, his guide, Big Vern, simply chuckled and said, "Guess we'll take the truck."

The truck, a rusted Chevy that smelled of gasoline and old fast food, rumbled southward with Balthazar shivering in the passenger seat. The man driving, whose vocabulary was limited to grunts and the occasional "yup," nodded in satisfaction when Balthazar handed over another gold coin in thanks. "Nice tip," the driver muttered, pocketing the coin as they pulled into a roadside diner.

Inside, the warmth was overwhelming, the air thick with the scent of butter and coffee. Balthazar, still adjusting to this frozen land, eagerly accepted a stack of steaming pancakes. When he attempted to pay with yet another gold coin, the waitress simply laughed and said, "Hon, you keep that. But if you're looking for work, we could use a dishwasher."

"I am on a holy mission!" he declared.

"Yeah, sure thing, sweetheart. More coffee?"

At a late-night campfire, Balthazar huddled among ice fishermen who shared cans of beer and regaled him with stories of the legendary "Michigan Dogman". The tale of a half-man, half-wolf creature lurking in the forests sent a chill down his spine. "This land is cursed with demons?" he gasped. His companions howled with laughter.

The next day, he hitched a ride with a snowplough driver named Earl. "Truly, you command a powerful beast," Balthazar told him. Earl, shaking his head, simply replied, "Whatever you say, bud. Buckle up."

As they neared the Mackinac Bridge, Balthazar gaped at the massive structure rising into the sky, its towers stretching toward the heavens. "What divine gate is this? Surely it marks the passage to a sacred land!" he exclaimed.

Earl let out a chuckle. "That's just the bridge to the Lower Peninsula, bud. Ain't nothin' holy about it, 'cept maybe when the wind don't knock ya clean off. Also, folks down there? We call 'em trolls – 'cause they live under the bridge. We Yoopers stay up here where it's real."

Balthazar crossed in awe, clutching his jar of frankincense tightly as the mighty suspension bridge swayed slightly under the weight of traffic. The great expanse of water below seemed endless, a cold and mysterious abyss. He murmured a prayer under his breath, convinced he was passing through some grand celestial trial.

Each stop along the way, he continued asking for "Bethlehem". Each time, someone corrected him: "No, no, you mean Frankenmuth."

After crossing the bridge, Balthazar found himself in an entirely new land – one with larger towns, busier roads, and an ever-growing sense of movement. He wandered from town to town, following vague directions from well-meaning strangers, convinced he was nearing his divine destination. Eventually, he found himself at a bustling roadside rest stop, where a friendly trucker took pity on him.

"You still lookin' for Bethlehem?" the trucker asked, eyeing Balthazar's robes and the jar of frankincense he held tightly.

"Indeed, noble sir," Balthazar replied. "The place of the divine child must be near."

The trucker grinned. "Well, I'll tell ya what, hop in. I'm headin' to Frankenmuth. If you're lookin' for holy stuff, that's about as close as you'll get."

Hours later, as the truck pulled into town, Balthazar gasped. The towering Bavarian-style buildings, the streets lined with twinkling lights, and the giant Christmas store – it had to be the sacred land he sought.

Stepping out of the truck, he inhaled deeply, taking in the scents of cinnamon, roasted nuts, and pine. Before him stood a grand temple of Christmas, its sign gleaming in the soft glow of holiday lights: *Bronner's CHRISTmas Wonderland.* It was overwhelming – the sheer magnitude of holy decorations, nativity scenes, and an entire section dedicated to incense.

He staggered inside, the warmth washing over him like the desert sun. A woman in a red vest approached him with a bright smile. "Welcome to Bronner's! Looking for anything special?"

Balthazar knelt before her, offering his jar of frankincense. "I bring this sacred gift for the King."

She blinked. "Oh, uh… wow, that's authentic! Where'd you get it?"

"From the lands of the East, where the star guided me."

She glanced at a coworker. "You know, we could put this in the display. Next to the nativity scene?"

"Great idea!" the other worker said. "Looks real."

Balthazar exhaled. His journey was complete. He had fulfilled his duty.

"Sir," the woman said gently, "Do you… have anywhere to go?"

Balthazar looked around at the glowing lights, the smiling families, the shelves of holy symbols.

"Yes," he said, standing tall. "I believe I shall remain in this land of wonder." The towering Bavarian-style buildings, the streets lined with twinkling lights, and the giant Christmas store – it had to be the sacred land he sought.

Balthazar, Employee of the Year

And so he stayed. Bronner's hired him for his "historical authenticity". He worked the nativity display, telling customers grand tales of the ancient world. He embraced Michigan life, learned the art of shovelling driveways, and grew fond of flannel shirts.

By the following Christmas, he had a nametag:

Balthazar – Incense Specialist.

He never did make it to Bethlehem.

But, in a way, he figured he had found something just as miraculous.

Every morning, he burned a bit of frankincense in the back storeroom. Customers would wander by, take in the scent, and feel something they couldn't quite describe. Peace. Warmth. Nostalgia.

And so, with his pasty in hand and a snow shovel slung over his shoulder, Balthazar walked home through the snow-covered streets of Frankenmuth, content that he had, at last, found his place in the world.

About the author
Rob Whaley was born in Indiana and now resides in South Central Michigan. He is a US Navy Submarine Veteran, and alumnus of Purdue University and North Central College. In addition to writing, Rob is an avid mountain bike and gravel bike rider.

The Mysterious Journey of a Soul

Caliman Florentina

Perched high on the rock, Lucia gazed out towards the vast expanse of the lake. In the distance, a solitary boat came into view, its helmsman barely distinguishable as a silhouette. Out of the blue, a rocky islet emerged in the middle of the lake, with a temple right at its core rising from the grey rock. A huge, rainbow-hued aura constantly emanated from the temple walls toward the starry sky. Above, the round moon delicately sprinkled diamond powder onto the water surface.

Concealed beneath her black hooded cloak, Lucia descended the stone-carved stairs that led to the lake shore. The boat glided like a moment of reflection over the vastness of the water, approaching the lakeside. In the night's stillness, the only sound that filled the air was the soothing gurgle of the water, brought forth by the rhythmic motion of the oars.

As Lucia stepped into the boat, she tried to discern the enigmatic visage of the boatman. Despite her efforts, he was keeping his profile hidden while guiding the boat back onto the lake. The man's arms pushing the oars seemed vigorous, but the woman found it difficult to guess his age. Engrossed in thought, he appeared disconnected from everything around him, as if only the boat and himself existed in the entire world. Maybe he is mute.

How much time passed before the boat reached the rocky shore of the island? To her, it was like an eternity. However, that was no longer of significance. What truly mattered was that she had finally reached the destination her heart had led her to, in search of the wise man who held the answer to her burning questions: *Who am I? Since God's image is in everyone, why aren't we all equally wise and powerful?*

179

Close to the temple, the angles, distances between the walls, and colours underwent a bewildering transformation, changing at a dizzying pace. Lucia turned her head towards the shore and noticed the boat turned into a fog, disappearing without a trace. In front of her, the door of the temple opened wide.

The interior revealed itself bathed in a violet glow originating from the crystal walls. Atop a central, polished stone altar, a swirling purple flame burned with a cold intensity. Twelve zodiac signs ringed the temple dome.

In front of the altar, a mage stood, appearing to be the very embodiment of Time, lost in contemplation. The silence was so profound that it defied the concept of sound, and time itself felt suspended in this tranquil space.

From his cloak, he withdrew a carved ampoule made of amethyst. With meticulous care, he poured its contents into a chalice crafted from jasper, which was filled with enchanted water. Magically, the water smoothly transformed, shifting from a violet-pink reminiscent of the Aurora Borealis to a golden yellow, before finally settling into a bright red like the blood.

As the mage glared into the chalice, the colours' metamorphosis revealed strange visions. In the pink water, two angels became visible, one with broken wings. Into the golden water, an image formed, showing an elderly king on his deathbed. And in the depths of the red water, flames from a roaring pyre soared into the sky.

Without looking back, he spoke. "So, I was not mistaken. You have arrived at last."

A torrent of questions rushed from the woman's lips, her eyes widening with curiosity.

"Do you know me? Have our paths crossed before? Were you expecting me? How did you know I was coming?"

The mage turned, and his violet eyes fixed on her.

Lucia saw an elderly man of timeless beauty, with a forehead graced by prominent wrinkles that reflected an entire era of wisdom. His gaze, calm yet not gentle, carried a distinct air of sagacity. With his long beard cascading down to his chest, he bore a resemblance to a sage from ancient times. The old man handed her the chalice of coloured liquid.

"There are too many questions being asked all at once. You will have enough time to uncover the truth, step by step. To begin with, drink this!"

Lucia gripped the chalice with both hands and took a sip of the potion. Within a brief span, her eyelids grew heavy and her senses surrendered to the embrace of a drowsiness with half-closed eyes, and vivid dreams came into life in front of her.

In the realm of the celestial, sunlight flowed like a waterfall over the stardust and the stars themselves were singing an ode to the universe. Ethereal beings, dressed in white frocks garnished with rainbow girdles, floated delicately on opalescent clouds. Like ants in an anthill, the angels scurried around, each with a distinct purpose. Some were tasked with conveying humanity's prayers to God, acting as messengers between realms. Others were entrusted with the important duty of guarding the destiny of Earth's inhabitants.

Amid this splendour, an angel stood tall, with eyes resembling the colour of amber. This was Lucifer, beloved by God, the angel to whom the Master of the universe could never deny a wish. From the lofty heights of Paradise, Lucifer glanced down, his attention being drawn to a woman on Earth.

Night after night, he would watch as she fixed her violet eyes upon the stars and sighed, murmuring: *I wonder how the world appears from up there.*

In those moments, he noticed his thoughts were turning into rhyming words.

Here am I, whispering your name
Please, cast your fears aside
I claim you as my twin flame
So, leave your world behind.

One day, as the most beautiful angel swept a glance to the Earth through the curtains of clouds, a longing stirred within its heart and mind.

"Oh Issa, you sweet creature, how I wish you were here!"

Almost instantly, he perceived her diaphanous silhouette in a group of joyful angels playing by tossing balls of light at each other, their laughter rolling in waves of love. He found himself unable to avert his gaze from the beautiful being, pondering whether her presence was real or a figment of his imagination.

Half-closed eyes, absorbed in his own musings, he gave tongue to his innermost thoughts about the maiden that had ignited his passion.

"I had no desires before I saw you, Issa. Yes, you awakened them all within me. Your hair shines like a tear of gold. A tiara made of stars would be a perfect fit for you."

The news, brought by an angel, interrupted his reverie.

"I have a mission from God, Lucifer."

"Ah, my loyal servant, Suryal. What is it?"

"I must collect stars from the sky to craft a tiara."

"A tiara? For whom?"

"For the beautiful maiden Issa."

Lucifer was so proud! As always, once the wish arose in his mind, the angels promptly arrived with news of its fulfilment. Immense gratitude filled him.

God has granted my greatest desire. I am blessed.

He paused, contemplating whether the simple fulfilment

of his desires might signify something more. In a sneaky manner, a thought crept into his mind and slipped out through his mouth.

"However, doesn't it imply that I am God's equal if all my wishes are instantly satisfied?"

Out of nowhere, a voice echoed like thunder behind him.

"Unfortunate you! What have you done? How can you even think of comparing yourself to Me, the Almighty, the unique Supreme Being of the Universe?"

The sky abruptly transformed, casting a shroud of darkness over the Heaven. Lucifer was forcefully pulled into a bottomless abyss by a strong suction, as though an invisible hand was dragging him there. While he was plummeting through the void, thousands of lightning bolts were chasing him, splitting the sky. The abyss roared and trembled with immense power, creating the illusion that Heaven itself was collapsing to Earth. Lucifer descended further, passing by dying stars, with thousands of years seeming to pass in the blink of an eye.

Soon after, the chaotic tumult slowly faded away, making room for a deep silence. In front of his eyes, a planet was growing bigger and bigger. Still descending through the dense clouds, he caught sight of mountain chains, their peaks reaching towards the sky. Below, glistening waters and sprawling fields garnished with fragrant flowers unfolded before his eyes. A thud... and, in an instant, his greatness became nothing but a deep darkness, like a dreamless slumber. The fallen angel was lying on a piece of land by the seaside. His last memory was of a maiden who had grown angel wings.

When Lucia regained consciousness, tears welled up in her amber-like eyes. She pressed one hand against her chest, trying desperately to ease the sharp pain piercing her heart. The mage's warm voice calmed her.

"That's all for now."

A swift movement of his hand told her to follow him. The mage then opened the door of a cell carved into the stone, unveiling a bed, a cupboard, and a table by a small window. A cup of herbal tea, a plate with two slices of honey coated-bread, and some fruit sat on the table.

"Make sure you eat something! It's important for you to regain your strength. Do you need anything else?"

"I need some answers. Who are you?"

"Allow me to introduce myself. Isaiah is my name, and I'm a mage."

"A mage! How did you uncover your true identity?"

"It was easy! Even as a child, I knew I wasn't like others. I had a persistent inner voice that answered any question I posed to myself. It was during one of these moments that I discovered I had actually reincarnated by my request to save someone. However, let's set that aside for now; all will be revealed in due time."

Lucia knew there were limits to what she could understand in a single day, but she longed to comprehend more. Alone in the little room, she rested her temples on her elbows, staring at the sky, consumed by a profound sense of sorrow. *Do fallen angels remain condemned for eternity? Will they ever be forgiven?*

The next day unfolded quickly, introducing a mysterious and tranquil evening. Like a golden shield suspended in the sky, the moon watched over the Earth in silence. Isaiah, the mage, gently rang a bell. Before Lucia could understand how he had entered her room, she heard his swift command.

"Come with me!"

Without saying a word, she followed him along a path that led deeper into the very bowels of the Earth. In the torchlight's glow, a cave materialized, its walls made from polished rock and the ground carpeted in black sand. At the heart of the cave, a massive amethyst crystal rested on a solitary stone pedestal.

The crystal suddenly pulsated, its hue changing. A beam of light emerged, rising like a sword blade until it reached the rocky ceiling of the cave. All at once, the ceiling split open, exposing the dark blue velvet of the sky. Against this backdrop, the ocean of stars shone coldly. The light extended even further into the outer space until merged with a star that surpassed all others in both size and radiance.

The colourful liquid Lucia sipped immersed her into a dreamy state where she perceived time becoming fluid. In the distance, the divine voices of an angelic choir were spreading their harmony through the air.

Three wise men from the Far East
Followed the Star, which guided their feet
And they travelled as we heard
Till they reached Jerusalem
There, as they briefly stopped
The star hid from their sight
So, they went asking around
Where could be the Saviour found?

As Herod lay on his deathbed, his head resting upon pillows, nightmares tormented him. What shadows crossed the mind of this unfortunate soul?

The song continued to ring in his ears.

News hit Herod like a storm
As he heard about the new-born,
Quickly he the wise men called
And that was he has them told:
Find me the little Lord
For I want to worship Him
Offering gold, incense and myrrh.

In the labyrinth of his dark thoughts, a glimmer of a memory surfaced, like a star in a foggy sky. The encounter with the three magi kept replaying in his mind. But he was floating in a total confusion. Had it truly taken place, or had he dreamed? It had occurred some time ago, but exactly when was it? And wasn't there another mage who had arrived afterwards? Yes, that youthful and enchanting mage with purple eyes. Why was he so familiar? There was something about those eyes that reminded him of a long-lost connection, but he couldn't quite figure out how it was formed and when it was lost. And the song defiantly lingered in his ears.

Shining bright above the Wise Men
The Star appeared once again
And it finally stopped upon
The place where the Baby's born.

Struggling, Herod rose from his bed and approached a mirror. It was the same mirror he once used to marvel at his own grandeur.

In a lugubrious voice, he let out a scream. "Demon, show me your strength!"

The reflection in the mirror appeared distorted, like the rippling surface of a lake disturbed by a stone. Faint sounds and voices were coming from behind it – echoes of crying, curses, fragile whimpers, and the thunderous clatter of horses.

"Kill all the children under the age of two!"

"Please, spare my child. I beg you to take my life instead."

"No, not my child… Oh God, have mercy!"

"Kill them all!"

"May you be damned, Herod!"

A voice cut through the din. "Herod, the time has come for you to pay for your deeds."

The mirror emitted a strange, boiling laugh.

"Hahaha! I'm waiting for you in hell."

Slowly the mirror became clear just as a final thought crossed Herod's mind.

"I am nothing but a shadow."

Darkness engulfed his soul while he caught sight of the Death's Angel approaching, and a sinister light gleamed in his amber-like eyes. The servants found him crouched on the ground in the morning. His face was pale with fear, his wide eyes fixed on something unseen.

Lucia was startled by a sharp, bell-like sound. A profound weakness coursed through her at the moment she opened her eyes. It felt like every drop of blood had been drained from her veins, and the sparkle in her eyes was slowly fading away. The mage spoke to her with gentleness.

"Enough for today. If you need anything, you can find me in my lab."

A little while later, Lucia walked into the lab and noticed the mage in the farthest corner. He was hunched over papers that were scattered across a large desk. The room was lit by only a few candles that cast dancing flames on shelves laden with hundreds of bottles and jars labelled with peculiar names – *Lavandula spica, Mimosa pudica, Narcissus poeticus, Mimulus moschatus, Laurus nobilis.* An iron table displayed neatly arranged retorts, spirit vessels, crucibles, and pipes. Yet what truly gave the room a mysterious touch was the ceiling painted with a map of the sky, complete with the names of constellations.

"May I help you in any way?"

"What happened to the baby born beneath that brilliant star?"

"Legend has it that one of the wise men, delayed by helping those in need, never arrived at the baby's worship.

Despite missing the chance to honour the Infant, he met Him again thirty years later, this time as a crucified Man."

"Why was He crucified?"

"To fulfil His destiny. He was the chosen one, destined to save the world."

"Who can be saved?"

"Anyone. But let's leave the discussion for another time. Now I have other things to do."

In the small room, the woman knelt down, bowed her head in supplication, and clasped her hands together in prayer. *Anyone can be saved*, she whispered to herself hopefully.

As the third day drew to a close, golden stars started shimmering on the blue canvas of the sky, like frail bundles of trembling rays. Isiah appeared seemingly out of nowhere inside, leaning close to Lucia's ear.

"It's time. Follow me!"

Lucia and the mage descended the stairs to the shore, arriving at a wooden bridge slightly submerged under the lake. At the far end of the bridge, a wooded island stood ready to welcome them.

Trunks of ancient trees were mirrored in the water, giving the illusion of sharing a common root – one trunk reaching the surface while another stretched down to the depths of the lake. The moon became obscured by dense, dark clouds, only to re-emerge later, shining through the clouds which had been rent asunder in streaks of silver. It was a warm night, fragrant with the heady scent of flowers that covered the island. Here and there, a cricket hoarsely chirped.

Once more, Lucia took a sip from the enchanted chalice, and soon she fell prey to a warm torpor.

The wandering mage strolled through the forest, a woven bag slung over his shoulder, containing his sole possession:

an old book. Once covered with gold leaf, now peeled in places, this ancient tome held the key to any mystery, bringing into light the nature of all things. A few alchemical symbols and the Latin title remained visible on the weathered cover. Star charts, mystical mathematics, magical invocations, herbal remedies, and dream interpretations were all found within its pages.

Trailing closely behind, a delicate young woman was carrying a small crate containing cures and potions. The female mage's knowledge and magical abilities created a powerful attraction for this orphaned girl, who became her devoted disciple. Irresistibly drawn into the realm of mysteries, the disciple's mind absorbed every word from her master.

"Well, Isabel, humans were created in the image and likeness of the Creator, and within them, the Universe is found on a much smaller scale."

"And how were they created?"

"In the beginning, light was created as an attribute of fire. Therefore, fire was the first element to be created. Following that, water, air, and finally earth appeared, leading to the creation of humans from the combination of these elements."

"What do these elements do in the body?"

"They assist in the composition, maintenance, death, and decomposition of the body, each playing a specific role under the laws of the universe."

"How can humans be aware of their own divinity?"

"By knowing oneself, one can understand the microcosm and, further, gain insight into the macrocosm."

"I see! The microcosm reflects the macrocosm."

"There are a few things that you should know. The first one is that your body holds the key to understanding yourself. Listen to your body! Let it express itself!

Collaborate with it! If you find disharmony, act on it! You can use magic for this."

"Got it! Body is important."

"Second, throughout the existence, mankind has held belief in a multitude of things: either they were ideas, actions, objects, fellow individuals, fallen angels or demons. However, it is imperative that mankind's faith ultimately rests with the Creator."

"Right! Faith should belong with the Creator."

"Third, we are both Death and Life. But do we know who we are?"

The mage, completely wrapped up in her own thoughts, was unaware of her surroundings. Enthralled by the mage's eloquence, the young disciple barely noticed they had reached the edge of the forest. A meadow stretched before them, like an enchanted garden from fairy tales, where colourful flowers basked in the warm embrace of the sun's nurturing rays.

The amber-like coloured eyes of the mage studied the soil and carefully plucked a plant before handing it to the disciple and explaining its magical properties.

"*Achillea millefolium* is ruled by the planet Venus and the element of water. Infusions prepared from the flowers of this plant should be drunk by the light of a purple candle to strengthen the capacity for clairvoyance."

"Achi… how?"

Isabel's eyes grew wide as she took in the overwhelming amount of information. The knowledge both thrilled and confused her. However, her fascination quickly turned to a fear that froze her blood in the veins when a group of armed men burst into their sight.

"Here you are! You are being arrested for witchcraft in the name of the Church."

With their hands bound and soldiers flanking them, the

mage and her disciple blazed their path into the village, walking through the crowd of furious faces. As they moved forward, all they could spot were mouths, twisted in grimaces, shouting and eyes filled with flames of hatred. The villagers' stares left no room for doubt that they had already deemed the two women guilty of causing the plague that ravaged their village, sentencing them to death.

The priest, village chief, and oldest villager were quickly summoned to the village square to create a panel of judges. False accusations rained down from all directions, growing more and more absurd.

"The witch promised to bring back my husband's love."

"She gave me venom to drink."

"I saw them dancing with the Devil."

The accusatory voice of the priest reverberated through the gathered crowd.

"You are being accused of witchcraft. What would you say in your defence?"

"I am not a witch, but a wandering mage coming from the majestic mountains named The Stone of the Mage King, in the enchanting land of Transylvania. My name is Danielle."

"A wandering mage? What's this?"

"A mage who wanders the world helping people. Some are guides or teachers sharing wisdom. Others possess the ability to heal people with magic. Through their interactions with others, they can also identify potential disciples. Isabel is one such disciple of mine."

"Mage or witch, the same thing."

"Not true. A mage is an apprentice in the realm of the great mysteries, while a witch knows only minor mysteries. A mage faces demons, rebellious angels, and renegade spirits. Witches use demon's power in their practices."

"Blasphemy! It is only the priests who possess the

ability to combat demons and emerge victorious with the divine help of God."

The accuser reached into Danielle's bag and pulled out the book, flinging it down with a look of contempt.

"Do you deny that this devilish book belongs to you?"

The crowd stirred, the noise quickly spreading around. The women, pious as ever, crossed themselves while the men raised their voices in a unified cry.

"Witches to be burned at the stake!"

While Danielle was trying to decipher on people's faces what they hid in their hearts, she met Isabella's eyes and noticed the terror reflected in them. Instantly, she made a swift decision.

"I must confess that I am a witch and I am prepared to face the consequences of my despicable actions. However, I plead for the release of Isabel, who is truly innocent. I cast a spell upon her and she was unaware of what she has done."

A soldier grabbed Danielle and tied the noose around her neck. The crowd's cry of death was unleashed more fiercely and more wildly as the hanged body swayed, enveloped in flames on the hastily erected pyre.

Evening had descended, yet Isabel's violet eyes remained fixated on the billowing smoke, ascending under the ethereal form of a woman.

"I'll always carry the burden of this sin. I couldn't save you from death, Master."

When Lucia's eyes fluttered open, her body quivered uncontrollably. The dream had been incredibly lifelike! Or perhaps it was more than just a dream. Could her eyes have unravelled the fabric of reality itself? Her eyes met the mage's eyes.

"What were those dreams all about?"

"To be clear, those weren't dreams; they were memories."

"Are you saying…"

"Yes. You witnessed your own fall and glimpsed your past lives as Herod and Danielle. Over countless lifetimes, your soul has travelled through various bodies, a concept the ancient Egyptians called metempsychosis. Our paths have intersected on multiple occasions, such as when I was Issa, one of the wise men or Isabel."

All of Lucia's past lives had flashed before her eyes like paintings, and a tear rolled down from her right eye for those lives lived in vain. Her lives were encapsulated in that tear. A single tear, akin to a precious crystal, that dropped into the enchanted chalice.

"I was the proud angel who believed himself to be God. I was also a tyrant, a beggar, a courtesan, a hangman. Will I be condemned eternally?"

"Don't be so harsh on yourself. You've also lived a life where you took upon yourself a sin that you did not commit and redeemed it through your own innocence."

"What options do I have?"

"The path up and down is the same, with only the direction changing. A fall is the consequence of pride; a rise is achieved through humbleness."

"I am still unsure about what I should do."

"Listen to the whispers of your soul, for the answer you seek lies within. There is an unimaginable power in those three simple words. But choose them wisely! Only three attempts are allowed."

"Three words! What could they be?"

"You can only find what you already possess within yourself. If it's not within you, it doesn't exist for you, and your search will be in vain. Never forget that the Creator's mercy reflects His love for all. He will patiently wait until the last fallen angel returns to Him."

With a deep sigh and eyes closed, Lucia hesitantly began her attempts.

"God, have mercy!"

As they carved their path in the ether, the three words left the imprint of hope in the woman's soul. Holding her breath, she waited for a sign from above, but nothing came. With each passing second, Lucia's hope faded, giving way to disappointment. But then she realized that mercy might not be the answer she sought. Summoning courage, she tried again.

"Forgive me, God!"

The same silence… the same stillness. Lucia pondered, *"Perhaps God's forgiveness alone is not sufficient. What must I discover within myself to regain Paradise? Whose forgiveness do I need the most?"* As the minutes melted away, the truth became clearer in her mind and an adamant certainty warmed her heart.

"I forgive myself!"

Lucia felt as if lifted by an unseen force as she embraced self-forgiving. She sensed her body becoming fluid, able to expand, shrink, and mould itself into different shapes. As her body became less dense, she felt lighter, yet stronger. Wings sprouted from her back, growing larger until she transformed into a glorious angel, none other than Lucifer. Blond locks fluttered around the angel's marble-white head while his amber eyes sparkled like the sun's tears. The long, white wings curved over his shoulders and a halo of blue stars shone on his forehead. The angel ascended on a radiant beam of light until he was blinded by a brilliance akin to the sun rising from all directions.

In the heavenly realm, in front of God's throne, Lucifer's eyes rested upon an entity with violet eyes exuding an indescribable splendour. A profound sense of joy flooded him.

"There is no place like Heaven! I would love to stay here for a little longer. However, who knows what lies ahead?"

About the author

Florentina Caliman is an engineer with a background in writing scientific papers so far. Her love for fairy tales, ancient history, and myths inspired her to venture into storytelling.

The Road Trip

Henry Lewi

In the Infinite Celestial Office on the very edge of Time and Space, the Chief Celestial Engineer and his infinite team of Celestial Mechanics had finally repaired the Universe. The result had been closure of the many wormholes and rips in the Space-Time Continuum of the Cosmos that had been developing ever since the Big Bang had occurred over thirteen billion years previously.

As a consequence of the repairs, much of the carefully ordered and beautifully shaped galaxies in the Cosmos had become somewhat distorted, flattened and misshapen but the repairs were complete, the Universe was now intact, the Infinite Celestial office had accepted it, and the Chief Celestial Engineer now signed off on the repairs. The all-powerful infinitely wise Celestial Chairman looked at the now repaired Infinite Universe and was satisfied. The Giant Omniversal Display known as the G.O.D., which constantly monitored the Infinite Cosmos, showed that all was now finally at peace throughout the Universe.

The original bagel-shaped Universe was now somewhat plumper, rounded and thicker, and as Lucifer the Chief Demon in the Celestial Office, and an expert in all things pastry based, described it as *"looking more like a jelly doughnut than a bagel"*.

"Time for a road trip I believe," said the Celestial Chairman. "I think we, three," pointing at himself, the Chief Celestial Engineer, and Lucifer, "should all go; its all's quiet at the moment, and the one place I'd really like to visit is that backwater planet that the locals call Earth, I understand the food's good, the wine excellent and the music so much better than that rubbish Gabriel is always playing on his Infinite Trumpet. What do you guys think?"

196

"Great idea," replied Lucifer. "Should we bring along the Legion of Demons for protection etcetera?"

"No, I don't think so," replied the chairman. "We'll keep the group small. We'll take Gabriel along who can always announce our presence with his Infinite Trumpet. Michael, who despite being an idiot, can always provide protection with his Flaming Sword, and The Archangel Metatron can organise, lead and record the trip."

And so it came to pass that in and around those infinite moments of time the All-Powerful Beings of the Infinite Celestial office began their Road Trip down on Earth.

They were announced as Three Wise Men called Shadrach, Meshach, and Abednego, as they walked through the Blue Gates of Ishtar and presented themselves to Nebuchadnezzar, who promptly threw the three of them into a burning furnace, no harm done obviously. They visited the court of Kublai Khan, where they were made most welcome; and in the court of Darius the Great in Ancient Persia they were received and anointed as the "Three Magi". In the Black Lands of Egypt they watched as the Great Pyramid of Giza was built. They stood amongst the crowd as Thomas Crafts read out the Declaration of Independence from the balcony of the State House in Boston, and were there when the Bolsheviks in Petrograd stormed the Winter Palace. They watched as the Montgolfier Brothers flew their hot air balloon at Versailles, and when the Wright Brothers flew the first aeroplane at Kitty Hawk. They were at Cape Canaveral when Apollo XI was launched, and they stood on the edge of the Sea of Tranquillity in the shadow of Planet Earth as The Eagle landed on the Moon. Some 250 years later they were observers as the first Interstellar ship, *The Miguel Alcubierre* was launched on its voyage of exploration and conquest.

The All-Powerful Celestial group rode motorbikes down on Route 66 as it wound its way from Chicago to LA, from St. Louis down to Missouri, and they all agreed that Oklahoma City looked oh so pretty!

They played the music of Canned Heat, Chuck Berry and Bob Dylan as they drove their open-topped cars down along the Pan-American Highway from Prudhoe Bay in Alaska to Ushuaia in Argentina and took the Trans-Siberian Express from St. Petersburg to Vladivostok, drinking black tea from Samovars as they smoked Papirosa, the Russian filterless cigarette.

Across the infinite arcs of time and space the Celestial Beings crossed and re-crossed the planet as they continued on their Road Trip.

On one dark night they rode their camels as they crossed the desert in the forgotten land of Judea, and Metatron pointed out the bright star he was using as a beacon to guide their journey as the group slowly made their way south towards Bethlehem.

"One last thing before we head home," said Metatron. "It's been fun hasn't it? Everybody happy?"

"Absolutely" said the all-powerful Celestial Chairman. "OK, time to announce our visit, and let's do it in style." He sent Metatron, Gabriel and Michael ahead. The three Archangels now rode their camels towards the small local inn on the outskirts of the town.

The Celestial Chairman, Chief Celestial Engineer and the Chief Demon Lucifer followed the sound of Gabriel's Infinite trumpet and made their way to the stable next to the Inn, where a large crowd had now assembled.

The Archangel Gabriel blew his trumpet three times, as Michael unsheathed his flaming sword, and both Archangels now stood either side of Metatron in front of the crowd, both with their wings stretched wide.

"Behold," said Metatron with his wings finally unfurled, as he now announced the arrival of the Celestial Chairman, the Chief Celestial Engineer and the Demon Lucifer. "Every valley shall now be raised up, every mountain and hill made low, the rough ground shall become level, the rugged places a plain. I now present to you, the three Infinitely Wise, Infinitely Powerful, Infinitely Patient, Lords and Kings of the Infinite Heavens. See, wonder, and marvel at their power, and their wisdom." The Archangel Metatron's announcement was made as Gabriel continued to quietly play his Infinite Trumpet. "Bring forth the child for the Celestial's blessing." A member of the gathered crowd struggled forward with a small baby in their arms, and the all-powerful Celestial Chairman now spread his arms and blessed the child.

"*Bit over the top*," mumbled Lucifer to himself.

"I think that went well don't you?" said the Celestial Chairman, sometime later as they all settled back into the calm of the Infinite Celestial Office.

"We'll see," replied Lucifer.

About the author
Henry is a retired surgeon and member of the Canvey Writers Group. He has published a number of stories on the *CaféLit* site.

The Second Coming

Yrev Very

Terapion, a monk, had once been a devout follower of Athanas. He was rough and severe in temperament. He came to Greece, intending to exorcise the land because the peasants there still believed in the spirits that dwelt among the trees and springs. And the pranks played by the fairies had brought numerous disasters to the local area, such as luring children to dance on the edge of cliffs, making livestock go missing, and causing young men to die as they followed them. Terapion adopted a series of drastic measures to confront the fairies. He cut down the phoenix trees where they often appeared, burned the olive trees and pine trees that might hide them, and erected crosses everywhere so that the little goblins would not dare to approach. Gradually, the village became a sacred place. Finally, they were forced into a cave in a desolate small valley. The monk Terapion was determined to wipe them out completely. So, on a night not long after Easter, he gathered his followers, brought tools and crosses, and came to the cave. He built a small chapel at the entrance of the cave, attempting to trap the fairies inside forever.[1]

That evening, Terapion saw a woman walking towards him along the path. She had her head bowed and was a bit hunched over; her coat and shawl were all black, yet through the dark fabric there emanated a mysterious faint glow, as if the morning light was shining there. Although she was quite young, she possessed the solemnity, slowness and dignity of a woman over seventy years old, and also

---

[1] The above story is from *The Chapel of Our Lady of the Swallows* by Marguerite Yourcenar.

gave off the fragrance of ripe grapes and fragrant flowers. She walked past the chapel and examined the monk carefully, disturbing the monk who was in the middle of praying.

"This path ends here, woman," he said to her. "Where are you from?"

"From a village further away, where the clouds are still shining brightly," the young woman replied. "What are you doing here, old monk?"

"I've blocked the fairies who were harassing this area in this cave," the monk said. "In front of the cave's exit, I built a small chapel. They dare not escape through here, for they are afraid to show their nakedness before God. When they starve and freeze to death in this cave, then God's peace will reign over the earth."

When the woman heard this, her eyes fixed on the monk. He felt infinite sadness flowing from them. "May these creatures, whom you consider useless and harmful, also receive God's grace. Passing through the village ahead, from time to time I hear women and children weeping softly for these fairies' unfortunate circumstances."

The red clouds faded away and, though there was no wind, the night that was about to replace the blue sky still seemed to be lingering on its way. The rising moon was the same colour as the white clouds. It was close to the autumn season, but the weather hadn't cooled down because of it. Terapion, who had been toiling for two days, now felt extremely stuffy and uncomfortable. Whenever he breathed a bit harder, his head would feel swollen and painful. The discomfort of his body and the woman's words slowed down his thinking.

The faint moans in the cave, which lacked the moisture, ceased. The once slippery moss on the rock surface was now listless and no longer looked the same. In a short while, it cracked and fell off layer by layer. The mountain where the white chapel was built was slowly being replaced by dead vegetation, just like all the creatures that couldn't receive the gospel, and became a barren land.

To conceal his growing uneasiness, the monk asked again, "Woman, why have you come all this way here?"

The woman said, "I received the news that my child, who died bearing sins, was to be resurrected on the third day after being entrusted to this cave. I never expected that before I could see my child, many more sufferers had been added to this cave."

The sorrowful woman with a pale face then walked straight towards the cave behind the altar. The panic-stricken monk Terapion instinctively stepped aside to make way.

As if a tiny pebble had been dropped into a vast bottomless abyss, the woman entered the cave silently and for a long time there was no sound coming out. The guilty monk finally convinced himself to turn around and grope his way forward bit by bit in the darkness. He saw that the white cross was still firmly blocking the entrance of the cave, and the Son of Man nailed to the cross had been taken down from the instruments of torture by his mother; Terapion stood in front of this white wooden frame that connected the inside and the outside, put his head closer to the inside and listened sideways. Faintly, he could only feel his own held breath exhaling and the headache caused by the pressure of his blood rushing through his veins and the violent thumping of his heart.

From that night on, the hot-tempered monk Terapion stayed on the lonely and inaccessible mountain and never appeared in people's sight again. And this barren and dilapidated highland seemed to be protected by a magical power and was getting farther and farther away from the inhabited areas. The desolate and forbidding barren mountain, where there was no flowing spring water nor the moisture of rain and dew, became a paradise for some creatures. For example, the white chapel was a good place for swallows with black wings to build their nests.

The migrating black birds always flew at night. The fleeting shadows disappeared even faster than the sounds they left behind. The bright and shrill cries always unexpectedly interrupted the meditation of the most diligent ascetics. With an unknown, sharp and brief uneasiness, they suddenly broke away from the tranquillity and returned to their original state. The ascetics had to wait, waiting for their mood to return to tranquillity. On the remote and desolate high mountain, after the white chapel had been waiting for a year, the black-winged birds finally came in flocks again. Amid their soft chirping, the birds looked for their desired mates to build nests together. With their chirping and chattering, they either repaired their old nests or built new ones, so that their chicks could live safely in the nests until they grew up and could fly.

About the author
Yrev Very (Chang Feichang) currently lives in China. This short story was originally written in Chinese and translated into English by the author himself.

They Came from the East Riding on Camels

Liz Cox

Pete and Colin were sitting on the bank of the canal poking sticks into the water when Pete turned to Colin and said, "Hey Colin, did you know the Three Wise Men were from Yorkshire?" Pete continued to poke the oily water, making swirls in the rainbow lights with his stick.

"Don't be an idiot Pete," retorted Colin, "how can they be? They went to see the baby Jesus in Bethlehem. Isn't that somewhere in the desert with sand?"

"That's true," said Pete, "but didn't Miss Morris tell us that the Bible says they came from the East Riding on Camels? The East Riding, that's us, isn't it? We're in Yorkshire, which means the *M-aaaa-giii* were also Yorkshire men like us. It's written down, it must be true."

"'Spose so." Colin sounded doubtful but continued to poke in the water narrowly missing a stickleback which had swum too close. "I've never seen camels around here though. Where did they get them from? I've seen horses at the racecourse, but never camels."

"Perhaps we're special here in Beverley and they have camels hidden behind the horses."

"I don't think so, but we can ask Miss Morris on Monday." Pete stood up and threw his stick into the water, causing the ducks to scatter and squawk. He wiped his hands on his jeans and picked up the half-eaten jam sandwich that was lying on the bank, dusted off the dirt and began to chomp on it. "This sandwich is a bit gritty, but it's OK. Do you want a bit?"

Colin shook his head and headed for the gap in the fence where they had accessed the canal bank.

"We can ask our Geoff about the camels. He told me

once that a farm shop in North Yorkshire had camels," said Pete.

"That's not East Yorkshire, though, is it? And they can't be the same camels because the Three Wise Men went to Bethlehem in the olden days. Those camels would be dead by now." Colin shook his head, as he lifted the barbed wire and clambered through the gap.

Pete followed him.

"Col," said Pete, "how do you 'spose they got across the sea to Bethlehem? Were there boats sailing to Africa then? Bethlehem's in Africa, isn't it?"

"Well, strictly speaking it's in Northeast Africa, in Palestine," retorted Colin, ever the pragmatist and the better student of geography. "That's what Miss says."

"OK, Northeast Africa then, but do you suppose they had boats that sailed there?" Pete rubbed his nose then whacked the nettles in the grass verge with his foot. "Miss said in our history lesson, that the Vikings sailed to *Constant-inople*, but they came after Jesus."

"Maybe they just followed the Star, that's what the Bible says. They saw the Star in the East and followed it to Bethlehem. And they brought gifts for the baby – gold, frankincense, and myrrh. Useless things really; they would have been better bringing it a snowsuit."

"Do you think they would find those things here in Yorkshire?" asked Pete.

"Dunno." Colin rubbed his nose. "They'd find gold. There's lots of that here. My mum has a gold wedding ring, and old Mrs Wainwright who lives down our street wears lots of gold bracelets and necklaces. She's got the most ginormous gold earrings jangling in her ears. There's plenty of gold."

Pete nodded, then looked thoughtful.

"OK, what about the other stuff? I've never heard of

frank-in-cense and *myrrrrhh*. Do you suppose they get them from the mines along with the coal? There are mines down the road in Selby."

"Don't be so daft." Colin took a swing at Pete who ducked. "Something else to ask Miss Morris on Monday."

The boys turned the corner into Pete's road. The streetlamps were just beginning to glow. They huddled under the lamp outside Pete's house and wrapped their arms around their chests and shuffled their feet.

"I'm going in now," said Pete. "It's parky out here."

"See ya tomorrow," shouted Colin as Pete unlatched the gate and sauntered up the path to the pebble-dashed house swiping his mother's gladioli as he went. "Don't forget to ask your Geoff about the camels."

"I won't," shouted Pete.

"Leave them flowers alone our Pete." A strident voice emanated from the now open front door. "What've they ever done to you."

Pete was sitting at the table eating his egg and chips when Geoff came home from work. Pete looked up as Geoff sat down opposite him with his own egg and chips. Pete waited for him to squirt tomato sauce on his chips before he spoke.

"Our Geoff, you know you said there were camels in North Yorkshire."

"Yes, our Pete, what about it?"

"Is that true?"

Geoff's face creased with suppressed laughter, and he gave his dinner more concentration than it warranted. Then, he put his fork down and gave Pete his full attention.

"Well, Pete, I did see two when I went over to the Lake District. We stopped at a farm shop and there were certainly camels in the paddock."

"Do you think that's where the Three Wise Men got

206

their camels to travel to Bethlehem? The Bible says they came from the East Riding on camels."

Geoff spluttered. "They could have done, I suppose, but it would be a long way for them to go. Perhaps they got them from nearer home."

"Yeah, perhaps they did. Do you think they have them at Beverley racecourse along with the horses?"

"Can't say I've ever seen them, but who knows?" Geoff went back to piercing his egg with a chip, splashing yolk all over the table.

Pete thought for a while. This was getting nowhere.

The next morning Pete waited for Colin by the garden gate. He had more questions; Colin might know the answer. He'd spent the evening after tea looking through all the books on his bookshelf, but nowhere did it give any answers to his questions. He'd found a picture of the Wise Men in his Children's Illustrated Bible. They didn't look as if they came from Yorkshire, but perhaps they'd bought new clothes at a market on the way. He waved when he saw Colin approaching.

"Hi, Col," he said. "Had any more thoughts about the Three Wise Men?" There was no answer from Colin, but the boys fell into step beside each other. "Col, do you suppose the Three Wise Men wore a flat cap and donkey jacket like our dads when they set out? I saw a picture in my Bible, and they had fancy robes on."

"Well, they'd need the cap and donkey jacket when they set off for sure. A scarf as well. Jesus was born at Christmas and it's cold here. Even snows sometimes." Colin swung his school bag around and almost hit the neighbour's cat which was sitting on the wall. The cat shrieked and fled.

The boys arrived at school and once assembly was over,

they thought it was time to tackle Miss Morris on the thorny issue of the Three Magi. Pete raised his hand.

"Miss Morris, you know you said that it's written in the Bible that the Three Wise Men came from the East Riding on camels."

"Yes, Pete," Miss Morris replied.

"Well, Miss, does that make them Yorkshire men and did they travel to Bethlehem from Hull? With their camels and their robes and their gifts for the baby Jesus?"

"That's an interesting idea there Pete, let me think about it." Miss Morris was playing for time.

"Well, Miss, there are camels in Yorkshire, Pete's brother Geoff says he's seen some," said Colin.

"I'm sure there are," Miss Morris replied, "but I'm not sure they would have been able to sail with their camels from Hull."

"But Miss, you said the Vikings travelled to the East, didn't you?"

"I did indeed," replied Miss Morris, "and it's a true fact that people travelled further in the past than we would think possible." Miss Morris ran her fingers under her collar.

"You alright Miss?" said Pete. "You've gone a funny colour."

"Yes, Pete, I'm fine." Miss Morris fanned herself with the attendance register. "Now we must look at the evidence. There are camels in Yorkshire, and Hull is a port in the East Riding. I don't think it would have been a port in Biblical times, but people did sail in and out of the east coast."

"OK, Miss, what about their clothes. In the Bible pictures they have robes on and funny hats, but I think they would have worn donkey jackets and flat caps because it's colder here," said Pete. "Do you think they bought their new clothes when they got to Palestine, because it's warmer there and they would have been roasting?"

"Well, they certainly would be too warm in the desert if they had woollen coats on. Plus, they might have wanted to blend into the background a bit, you know, look like locals." Miss Morris was entering into the spirit of the thing now.

"And the gifts, Miss. Do you think they bought them locally when they got to the East? You know, to save them getting lost or damaged on the way," said Colin. "Besides, I've never heard of frankincense and myrrh. My mum said they don't grow here, at least she's never seen them in her gardening catalogue, and she knows everything about gardening does my mum."

"Good point, Colin," conceded Miss Morris, sweat now beading her brow. "I think we should put this to a class vote. So, class, do you believe that the Three Wise Men were from Yorkshire, based on the evidence put before you?"

The class had been sitting quietly for a change to the relief of Miss Morris. Now a sea of hands rose into the air. Wendy, a thin girl with red plaits, stood up. "No doubt about it miss, Pete's right." She grinned at Pete who was now standing up in front of his fellow pupils. He fair glowed with pride or was it bashfulness?

"Thanks, everybody. You can't argue with what's written in the Bible – Three Wise Men came from the East Riding on camels – they just had to adapt themselves when they arrived in Bethlehem. The Wise Men were Yorkshire men."

About the author
Liz writes short stories and poetry and is still finishing her first novel. She lives in North Yorkshire and at the time of writing is looking out at the darkness beyond her window.

Three Wise... Monkeys?

Sarah Swatridge

"I still can't believe it!" Mel said for what must have been the hundredth time. "Out of all the Women's Institutes and thousands of members, we've been chosen."

"I think one of the reasons was because we're known to be discreet," whispered Mrs Caspar with a knowingly look.

"You're right." Mel lowered her voice. "It's just so exciting!"

"I agree. It's not every day you go along to your monthly meeting expecting a slide show of someone's quirky musical boxes and end up finding yourself on an all-expenses paid journey of a lifetime." Balty laughed.

"Personally, I'd rather know exactly where we're going. The instructions are far too vague for my liking," Mrs Caspar added.

"Don't worry Mrs C," Balty said. "I've downloaded the *Follow the Star App*. I guess it sounds a bit hazy but I'm told, we'll know it when we see it!"

Their brief had been to travel as soon as possible, but in reality, a woman doesn't just grab a suitcase and walk out the door. Instead, she fills the freezer with a month's supply of homemade, nutritious meals that only need to be heated in the microwave. That, and all the necessary visas and formal paperwork took longer than expected. It was several days before they were ready to depart.

At the airport, Mel nudged Balty when they were given more information regarding their destination.

"Is it safe?" Mrs Caspar was asking.

"Have faith," said the man who'd handed over the envelope with their tickets. A moment later he'd disappeared into the crowd.

It was then they realised their flight had been delayed due to bad weather. They'd had a sprinkling of snow, but that was enough to cause chaos.

Eventually they boarded their flight to Tel Aviv. The three women wisely kept quiet. They listened more than they spoke. When one slept, the others kept alert, taking it in turns to have a nap. Mel was reminded of the Three Wise Monkeys, see no evil, hear no evil, speak no evil.

"I know we were told we'd be met at the airport, but I hadn't envisaged it would be by three camels," Mel said, her enthusiasm waning.

"The instructions suggest we've got quite a long ride ahead, which may take several days, so I think we ought to get started."

"But it's getting dark." Mrs Caspar reached for the envelope she'd been given. Surely, she'd mis-read something.

"I distinctly remember it saying about travelling by night because it's so much cooler, and safer too," Balty added.

"Really?" Mrs Caspar pulled her head scarf up around her face.

"Oh! Come on, it'll be fun. I've never ridden a camel before." Mel laughed. With that she gingerly approached one of the camels. They were huge up close but each of them had an air of confidence about them. These were three wise camels who obviously knew the area much better than they did.

The flight from Gatwick to Tel Aviv was only around five hours, but it was enough for each of the women to pick up some basic Arabic on Duo Lingo. They were intelligent women after all.

"That was easier than I thought," Mrs C admitted, having mounted her camel with her usual elegance.

Using the App, they began their journey out of the city.

It was obvious which star they needed to follow; it was the biggest and brightest one in the sky, even the camels seemed to understand where they were heading.

It was about thirty-five miles from Tel Aviv to Bethlehem but they weren't the only traffic heading that way. As luck would have it, there was some sort of Census going on and, unlike in the UK, where you just noted where you slept on Census Day; here you had to travel back to the place of your birth. Unless of course, you were a married woman, and then you went to your husband's place of birth. No surprise there!

"That's the tenth Airbnb I've tried. They're all full. It's the same with the hotels and guest houses. It might have to be the Youth Hostel."

"That'll be fine. All we need is somewhere to sleep, have a shower and a decent meal. We'll be on our way as soon as it gets dark." Mel rubbed her eyes. She was tired but didn't want to miss a moment of this adventure.

"Actually," said Mrs Caspar, "I'm sure I've got an old university friend who lives out here. I can message her on Facebook and see if she can help us out."

"Is that wise?" Balty asked. "I mean, under the circumstances?"

"Probably not," Mrs Caspar conceded. "She was an awful cook anyway. We're probably safer at the Youth Hostel."

The accommodation was basic but satisfactory. The worst thing was, having dismounted their camels, they found their thighs ached like nothing they'd ever experienced before.

"Forget the shower," Mrs Caspar said. "What I really want is a long soak in a hot bath with lots of Epsom Salts. Is that too much to ask?"

"It might be stretching it, but we can mention it on Trip Advisor when we write our review."

"Are you lost?" Mel asked the gentleman who she caught hanging around outside their room. She stepped

212

outside, pulling the door to their accommodation closed behind her so he couldn't see inside. After a few minutes, she returned looking a bit flustered.

"What was that all about?" Balty wanted to know.

"He said he was from The Herald; at least I think that's what he said. He wanted to know what we were looking for and if we'd found it? I didn't like the look of him. His eyes were too close together and his finger nails were grubby. I told him we're Spice Merchants. We'd come to visit the spice markets and were delighted to find so many different types of turmeric. I began to tell him about our favourite recipes but his eyes glazed over, just like my husband's do when he pretends, he's listening. After a minute or two, he muttered something and disappeared. Hopefully, we've seen the back of him."

The following evening, the sun had barely set, but the women were heading for the stables where they'd left their camels.

"They all look alike." Mel gasped as she searched the herd.

"I think our caravan is over there." Mrs Caspar pointed to three camels tethered to a wooden fence.

"For a moment then, I thought you'd found a caravan for the final stage of our journey. I was instantly thinking of making a brew and opening the tin of flapjack I've made."

"The collective noun for a group of camels is a caravan. Or a flock, but that just sounds wrong. Come on, let's get going," Mrs Caspar said and was pleased to see that the camels seemed to recognise them.

"Should we ride side saddle today?" Mel suggested but soon found she kept slipping and despite the unladylike position, decided to straddle the camel instead. "At least it's not such a long journey today. We'll be there by midnight."

"This can't be right!" Mrs Caspar said when the inn keeper led them round the back, taking their camels in one direction and pointing at a stable, gesturing that they should go inside. "Look at the state of this place!"

"Oh no!" Mel gasped as they heard the unmistakable cries of a newborn babe. "It seems we're a bit late."

"And you must be Mary?" Mrs Caspar introduced herself and her fellow WI ladies. "You're looking remarkably well, despite the surroundings, although I don't know what your mother would have said! But, have no fear, we're here now!"

Immediately the young man, Joseph, standing protectively behind Mary was sent out to fetch something for them to sit on. Balty ushered the shepherds, and their animals, out into the yard while they got on with a quick spring clean.

Mel was a nurse and had done a term of midwifery training. Discreetly she checked mother and baby were both in good health.

By the time Joseph returned, there was a lamb casserole simmering away over a firepit and the stable had been decorated with crocheted bunting.

"Joseph, I'm very impressed by your woodwork skills," Balty was saying as she inspected the little wooden cot and the rocking donkey that the baby would sit on when he was older.

"We too come bearing gifts!" Mel excitedly began to unpack one of their backpacks. "We had a collection and got you some vouchers – they're in the lovely gold envelope."

"Then I chose a few oils to pamper you, and the baby too," Balty handed over some beautiful glass jars. "Baby Massage is all the rage these days, and I just love a simple foot soak, especially with all this sand around. It gets everywhere."

"Rhythm Sticks – our knitting group, have been busy making baby clothes for a hot climate that gets chilly at night. There's practically every shade of blue, as we knew you were having a boy, although Mrs Thomas was a bit doubtful, so she's done lemon," Mrs Caspar explained.

"The casserole's ready," Balty announced. "It only needed to be heated up. We came prepared. Shall I serve the shepherds first as they're out in the cold?"

"Good idea," Mel said. "I'll give you a hand."

"Now," said Mrs Caspar to Mary, "If you like, we can babysit so you and Joseph can go out for the evening and have a bit of time to yourselves? You never know when you'll next get a chance."

Outside there was a lot of cheering and laughter. The shepherds, and their animals returned to the warmth of the stable. It seemed they'd had a sweepstake and the results were about to be announced.

It was clear that not everyone was happy. The sweepstake didn't have the usual odds because they already knew the baby was going to be a boy; furthermore, his name had already been chosen. So, the only things they could bet on was the date and the weight and, embarrassingly for their three guests, also the date of their arrival. How were they ever going to live it down that they were twelve days late for the birth?

About the author

Sarah Swatridge writes short stories for women's magazines worldwide. She now has a collection of twenty uplifting short stories called *Feel-Good Stories* along with her large print novels available in libraries and online. Head for www.thebridgetowncafebooksshop.co.uk/2024/08/feel-good-stories-by-sarah-swatridge.html for *An Honourable Wager*, *Feel-Good Stories* and lots more besides.

Visit www.sarahswatridge.co.uk and sign up to her monthly one-page newsletter.

Travelodge Epiphany

Penny Rogers

Angel #784 had been given an important task. He had accepted it gladly; successful completion would considerably enhance his standing on the celestial ladder, but he also knew that failure would mean another slide back down the rankings. Not so long ago he'd plummeted to #999, narrowly avoiding becoming a fallen angel, when he'd interfered in a human problem. Now, thanks to hard work and keeping his head down, he had begun the long climb back into favour. He really needed to get this job done properly.

On the face of it, it seemed quite simple. Get three rich men to the Travelodge on the outskirts of Wincanton on January 6. They were supposed to bring presents suitable for a baby boy. The angel thought this had all been done some two thousand years ago, but orders had come through from as high as it gets that it had to be done again.

The three men he had been tasked to approach were a Premier League manager, a DJ/Rapper and a hedge fund manager. All three proved very difficult to get hold of, even for an angel with special powers. The football manager was just too tied up with how his team were (or increasingly were not) performing and the rapper was busy headlining festivals or DJing at celeb-filled parties. As for the hedge fund manager, he was either drinking champagne in a VIP lounge at a racecourse or schmoozing clients in luxury hotels all over the world.

A possible solution to the problem presented itself one evening when Angel #784 was trying to call Ron, the football supremo. He'd actually got through, but been met by some very rough expletives and the sound of the handset being thrown across the room. He was on the point of giving up, going to THE BIG BOSS and admitting defeat, when he heard a soothing female voice with a charming accent that he took to be middle European, speak to him. "Good evenink. Zis is Kozi. How can I help you?"

It transpired that Kozi van Toots was part of Ron's entourage, and that she was getting fed-up with being eye candy for a workaholic football manager. She explained to the angel that Ron's short fuse was because he was aware that he'd seen his best years at the top of this very competitive ladder and didn't know what to do next. Over the course of a very long phone call, Kozi explained that she had grown up on a farm in a country that no longer exists and was no stranger to hard work. She had two degrees in biomedical engineering and had been in line for a research post at University College London. Then a model agency had spotted her, offered her more money than she had ever dreamed of, propelled her onto the catwalk and ultimately onto Ron's payroll.

"Am I right in thinking that you would like a challenge?" Angel #784 came straight to the point.

"Is it legit?"

"Completely legal. You can be assured of that. From the highest authority. Can you get to Wincanton in January?"

With Kozi on board, the angel decided he'd try a different approach to his problem. It did cross his mind to clear his idea with THE BIG BOSS but decided to go ahead and see how it turned out. So his next step was to visit the charming Cotswold home of the widowed mother of Edward Cholmondeley-DuPont-Waffletezer, the wealthy hedge fund manager.

In her stylish lounge, Stella was striding up and down in a state of frustration and anger when Angel #574 appeared one Saturday afternoon. She invited her unusual visitor to sit down on one of the elegant settees and explained that her wretched son Teddy had done it again: forgotten her birthday, not arranged to have her new Range Rover delivered, and was associating with completely the wrong sort of people. Teddy was just too wealthy, she surmised, and she was fed-up with sorting out the messes he made with whatever he did.

"Why do you help him?" The angel made himself comfortable, folding his wings as neatly as possible against the luxurious furniture.

"Well, I helped his Papa. Always did his accounts, all the financial stuff. When he died and left it all to Teddy, I just kept doing it. But I am going to stop. Let him find out the hard way. He'll probably ruin it all." Stella sighed. "But I want to do something worthwhile. Work for the Red Cross or similar."

This was music, heavenly music, to the ears of Angel #574. His idea was working out better than he had dared hope. He considered running his revised plan past THE BIG BOSS but instead said, "Would you be able to go to Wincanton on January 6?"

Steff-Anni had been quite a name a few years back. She'd been a talented musician and song-writer, and had even been nominated for a MOBO award. Then she married Justin (better known as DJ Eatabix) and had the children, so she had turned her hand to running a promotions business: finding models, locations, musicians, even cute animals for anything from consumer adverts to YouTube to corporate promotions. This worked well with family life and Eatabix's unpredictable working pattern. Steff-Anni had her hands full, so her first thought when Justin asked her to stand in for him on January 6 to help out a bro in a long white coat she said, "No, not possible, what about the girls?"

"You could ask your mum to look after them."

"Or you could ask her?"

"It'd be better coming from you, Babe. Tell her she can have some tickets for any show she fancies."

"OK, I'll do it. Just this once, mind you. Her flight to Lagos isn't until January 12. I'll text her later. Now, where, or what, is Wincanton?"

From his heavenly viewpoint Angel #784 flapped his wings in celebration. It didn't even cross his mind to explain his revised plan to THE BIG BOSS, who was of course fully aware of what was going on. If the angel had not been so focussed on getting the three women to Wincanton, he would perhaps have realised that THE BIG BOSS was not impressed with all this premature, and completely unnecessary, wing flapping.

Stella had been the first to arrive at the Wincanton Travelodge. She wasn't sure how the satnav in her new Range Rover worked, and she'd got lost somewhere on the Somerset Levels. However, by some miracle a sort of star had appeared on her satnav that eventually led her to an industrial estate on the outskirts of a small town. It didn't occur to her that the strange man in a long white coat, who had made himself comfortable in her lounge and talked her into doing this, had anything to do with the star on her satnav that guided her to her destination.

The other journeys weren't as straightforward. Kozi had got as far as Yeovil on the train, but was horrified to find that there were no taxis available for at least two hours. She was cold and wet, and very thankful that she'd selected Nike trainers over the Jimmy Choos for the journey. Standing outside the station, wondering how anyone ever got to their destination from this place, she recalled her childhood home. There someone would offer you a lift, even if it was on the back of a moped or in a cart along with a calf and a sack of fertiliser. Angel #784 tried to help by shimmering his wings; he'd realised that too much flapping would draw unwanted attention in his direction, just as everything was falling into place.

"You OK Miss?"

Kozi jumped. A man in a scruffy van stopped in front of her. She replied, "Um… how do I get to Vincanton pliz?"

"No idea. I could take you to **W**incanton, though."

"Zat is ver' kind of you. But…" Kozi looked warily at the untidy van and the male driver. Was it safe?

"Ahh, I see. I'm not going to hurt 'ee, and I'm a good driver. Look. I'll take 'ee to Winky, but first you call yer mum, or yer friend. Tell 'em what's goin' on and give 'em a picture of my number plate."

It was starting to snow so Kozi did what the man suggested and sent all the details to her sister Paula, then got into the ramshackle van. As she lurched and bumped her way to her destination she decided she would say goodbye to Ron and go back to her research. High above them, in the snowy sky, Angel #784 smiled.

Steff-Anni got a lift with a sound engineer who was visiting his parents in Tisbury, about twenty miles from Wincanton. He had offered to take her all the way there but she declined, thinking she could easily get a bus or a taxi. The cab she eventually found was very expensive, and refused to bring her back any later than 9.30 that evening. She declined the driver's rather grudging return service, thinking she'd sort something out even if it meant staying the night in the Travelodge. She was the last to arrive, and the three women met for the first time late on a freezing afternoon outside the budget hotel.

As they wondered what to do, a tall man in a long white

coat approached them. Stella recognised him from her lounge; the others hadn't met him before but after such an arduous journey they were simply relieved to have reached their destination. Afterwards their recollections of the evening varied, but there was a consensus that the man appeared to float rather than walk. His progression about twenty-four centimetres above the ground made him look even taller. His coat seemed to fit badly around the shoulders, as if he had something inside it. When he spoke, the words seemed to come from a long way off.

"We have to go elsewhere. They aren't here anymore. The council have given them somewhere to live." The exhausted trio looked at him with disbelief. The presents that they had brought with them: a casserole ready to pop in the oven, a large bag of disposable nappies and a musical merry-go-round, felt heavy along with their drooping eyelids. They all got into Stella's Range Rover and the strange man in a long white coat directed them to a small village about five miles away. They pulled up outside a rather gloomy looking terrace house in a side road. No street lamps or other lights, apart from an illuminated Santa suspended from an upstairs window next door, permeated the gloom. The tall man took them into the house, where there was a girl with a small baby and an old man in the background.

"It's very dark. Could someone switch a light on?" Stella asked as she trod on something soft and unidentifiable. "And cold. Too cold for a baby." No one answered.

"Smells bad too." Steff-Anni wrinkled her nose and rummaged in her bag for a tissue.

"At least zer are no animals," observed Kozi, but was then aware of a scurrying behind the dilapidated sofa.

The old man introduced himself as Josef and said the young woman was called Maria and that she was someone he'd met in the Salvation Army shelter. He explained they couldn't use too much electricity because they were on a pre-payment meter. There wasn't much credit left and they couldn't top it up because the nearest shop was in a village three miles away.

"And we've only got £7.84 between us." Josef admitted.

"That's not enough. How will you get there?" Stella was concerned.

"Don't know. There isn't a bus. I'll have to walk. Might get a ride." Josef sounded doubtful. Privately Stella thought it unlikely that anyone would give this scruffy man a lift. So she took charge.

"Right. We'll have a whip round, then I'll take you," she looked at Josef, "to this shop, top-up the electricity and buy some essentials. Meanwhile you two," this time she addressed Kozi and Steff-Anni, "try and clean this place up a bit and put that casserole in the oven for when we get back."

Steff-Anni was cuddling the baby. "Just as well I brought those nappies. Could you get some wipes at the shop?"

Maria and Josef stayed together, looking after the baby and just about managing in the dingy house. The council moved them again after a couple of weeks to a different village, where Josef was able to get a job. It was with a company that specialised in bespoke wooden furniture.

As a result of that night, the three women became firm friends and set up a WhatsApp group to keep up to date with the rural regeneration project that Stella was managing, Kozi's research at UCL, Steff-Anni's business along with her family life and work as a mentor for the King's Trust.

When it was all over, Angel #784 was called to another difficult meeting with THE BIG BOSS, who was not pleased that his instructions had not been followed to the letter. However THE BIG BOSS looked favourably on the sensible presents that the women had brought for the baby and the practical help they'd given to the struggling family.

The angel's punishment was to do some very boring statistical analysis of the international sale of Christmas cards with religious compared to secular themes, and spend some time mending halos that had been damaged by solar flares. But overall he felt that this time he'd got off quite lightly.

POST SCRIPT

When the next list of celestial rankings was published, Angel #784 was delighted to see that he'd been promoted to #665a.

About the author

Penny Rogers writes mostly short stories and flash fiction, is a regular contributor to CaféLit and has had stories in the Bridge House anthologies. Her writing has also been published in *Spillwords, Funny Pearls and Bare Fiction, Writers Forum* and in *SOUTH Poetry Magazine.* She has been runner-up in the Mani Literary Festival competition and was once short listed for the Bridport Prize for flash fiction.

Penny's collection of interwoven short stories *Amelie at the Window*, about a small town in France at the outbreak of WWI and afterwards in 1924, was published by Bridge House Publishing in October 2025.

When she's not writing, Penny enjoys preserving fruits and vegetables from her garden and visiting historic buildings. She is particularly fond of old churches and is inspired by their history, architecture and continuing contribution to their communities. She is especially good at sitting in her beautiful garden, advising the gardener (!) and planning her next story.

Index of Authors

Like to Read More Work Like This?

Then sign up to our mailing list and download our free collection of short stories, *Magnetism*. Sign up now to receive this free e-book and also to find out about all of our new publications and offers.

Sign up here:
http://eepurl.com/gbpdVz

Please Leave a Review

Reviews are so important to writers. Please take the time to review this book. A couple of lines is fine.

Reviews help the book to become more visible to buyers. Retailers will promote books with multiple reviews.

This in turn helps us to sell more books… And then we can afford to publish more books like this one.

Leaving a review is very easy.

Go to https://amzn.to/4nBbTu5, scroll down the left-hand side of the Amazon page and click on the "Write a customer review" button.

Other Publications by Bridge House

Good News...?
edited by Debz Hobbs-Wyatt and Gill James

Oh, be careful what you wish for.

One person's good news might be someone else's bad news. And if you do get what you wished for you might not be getting what you need. Or, if you're slightly more fortunate, you may no longer have anything to grumble about. These stories challenge the notion of what is good news and yet leave us still a little optimistic.

An amazing group of writers set the record straight in Bridge House's anthology *Good News....?*

Order from Amazon:

Paperback: ISBN 978-1-914199-88-2
eBook: ISBN 978-1-914199-89-9

Gifted

edited by Debz Hobbs-Wyatt and Gill James

What does it mean to be gifted?

Is this to do with a present being wrapped up and handed to another? Does one person sacrifice something to help someone else? Or is to do with having a certain talent? Is that gift always welcome? Does the protagonist make the most of what has been gifted to them? All of those scenarios exist in these stories and there are other interpretations as well of the theme "gifted".

Gifted is Bridge House's 2023 anthology which includes stories by both some of the gifted writers we already know well and by some new faces.

"A great selection of stories by some talented writers"
(*Amazon*)

Order from Amazon:

Paperback: ISBN 978-1-914199-50-9
eBook: ISBN 978-1-914199-51-6

Evergreen

edited by Debz Hobbs-Wyatt and Gill James

Life goes on. There is renewal. Nature endures.

This is a collection of challenging and thought-provoking stories. All stories have an everlasting message and these provide ones that will astound and delight you. We looked for: story, good writing, interpretation of theme and professionalism. All of the stories submitted had those elements. Here we offer a variation to cater to our readers' eclectic tastes. Sit back and surrender to the Bridge House magic.

Evergreen is a themed multi-author collection from Bridge House Publishing.

Order from Amazon:

Paperback: ISBN 978-1-914199-36-3
eBook: ISBN 978-1-914199-37-0

www.ingramcontent.com/pod-product-compliance
Lightning Source LLC
Chambersburg PA
CBHW072234170626
46813CB00003B/1222